AN ADVANTAGEOUS MARRIAGE

Alice Chetwynd Ley

AN ADVANTAGEOUS MARRIAGE

Published by Sapere Books.

20 Windermere Drive, Leeds, England, LS17 7UZ,
United Kingdom

saperebooks.com

ISBN: 978-1-912546-99-2

Chapter I

Lydeard Hall stood somewhere between the two modest villages of Great and Little Lydeard, sheltered among the round contours of the Chiltern Hills in an area of gentle, quiet beauty, crossed by small streams and rich in magnificent beechwoods.

The original house has been built in the fourteenth century by the first Baron Turville. Since then, successive generations had with unabating zeal pulled down and rebuilt it in accordance with the fluctuating whims of architectural fashion, leaving the present Baron with an elegant Georgian mansion in the classical style fronted by an impressive Ionic colonnade.

Not content with improvements to the house itself, the present owner's grandfather had called in no less an expert than Capability Brown to landscape the grounds. The result had been gratifying to the eye, if not to the purse. Clumps of fine oaks, elms and beeches had been grouped about the park to give variety to what must otherwise have been commonplace expanses of lawn. Any supposed deficiencies in natural beauty were screened from the eye by banks of thick shrubs and evergreens disposed with seeming casualness. But undoubtedly the masterpiece of the whole confection was the lake — an artificial lake which contrived to look as if placed there by Nature's own hand. Even a marble temple standing on a small island in the centre of the lake was not generally considered to mar the natural effect. It was all charming, quite charming, as lady visitors always declared when escorted over a delicately arched bridge to the temple by some male member of the household.

With never a discordant note in their environment, it might have been supposed that the occupants of the house would lead a similarly harmonious existence. This was not so, however. The melancholy fact was that the Turville family could rarely come together under one roof without some unpleasantness ensuing. Fortunately, visits from the younger generation to their parents were rare. The Honourable Francis Turville lived in London, as did his younger brother Aubrey. They were not obliged to see each other there, as their interests and friends were very different, Francis being a prominent member of the Corinthian set, while Aubrey detested all forms of sport and set himself up as something of a dandy.

The youngest member of the family, Lucilla, also lived in Town, but showed no more inclination for family gatherings than did her brothers. Four years ago in her first London season, Lucilla had delighted her mother by making a brilliant match with a wealthy Earl some fifty years her senior. Lord Ruscombe had doted on his eighteen-year-old bride, and had been so accommodating as to leave her a widow at the age of twenty. After a decent interval of mourning, the Countess had re-entered on the London social scene. Her cool, blonde beauty, and considerable fortune at once attracted plenty of admirers, but so far she had resisted all lures to embark on a second marriage.

No great matrimonial hopes had ever been entertained for Emmeline, six years older and a great deal plainer than her sister. It had been a relief to Lady Turville to see her eldest daughter married at all, so she had no fault to find with the stolid and unenterprising Joseph Welwyn, a squire living in a neighbouring county. The couple had been married now for seven years and had settled down well enough together. Joseph might be lacking in initiative, but his wife had more than enough force of character for both of them. She pursued his interests and managed his estate with an energy which even her rapidly filling nursery could not diminish. Never an affectionate female, the only interest she ever showed in any member of her family was directed towards her brother Aubrey, her junior by five years. Francis, with the unwelcome candour which he deliberately practised towards his family, said that this was because Aubrey, a weakly specimen in childhood, had always toadied to his elder sister. It was certain that Francis himself could never have been accused of this; during their childhood and adolescence, scarcely a day had passed without these two becoming embroiled in a quarrel.

In spite of their dislike of family gatherings, three out of Lady Turville's four progeny were reluctantly sharing the shelter of their parents' home on a fine day in the early Spring of 1816. They had presented themselves at Lydeard Hall in response to a peremptory summons from their mother which, for their different reasons, they had chosen not to ignore. Their sister Lady Ruscombe had evidently failed to feel the same compulsion, for she had conveyed her excuses. It might have been supposed that this defection would have added warmth to Lady Turville's reception of her more amenable offspring; on the contrary, it had put her out of charity with them all.

'It is all of a piece with the rest of her conduct!' she declared. 'She has not the least family feeling, and never does the slightest thing to oblige me!'

Francis, a dark, well-built young man in his middle twenties, raised a cynical eyebrow. 'Oh, I don't know, ma'am. She married Ruscombe to oblige you, what?'

'No such thing!' His sister Emmeline elevated her beaky nose in disdain. 'Lucilla was no martyr in that affair, as you very well know, Frank. She took Ruscombe because she wanted to — she'd angled for him hard enough!'

'And who is to blame her?' demanded Aubrey, who had a very slight lisp. 'I suppose a female must make the best match she can for herself.'

'The best she can — to be sure,' replied Francis, with a malicious side glance at his sister.

He saw from her quick flush that the hit had gone home, but she pretended not to have understood.

'That's all very well, but she was more than half promised to Peter Martyn.'

'Pooh, a boy and girl nonsense!' exclaimed Lady Turville, dismissively. 'But I wish you will stop brangling, and attend to what I have to say to you. Your cousin Eugenia will be with us tomorrow, and it's as well that you should know something of her history, before she arrives. My letters to you were necessarily brief, and I dare say you remember little of the circumstances of that affair from the past, for your father and I rarely spoke of it.'

'We all know that our father's younger brother blotted the escutcheon by marrying into Trade,' offered Francis helpfully. 'And that now you, ma'am, appear to think it a good idea for one of us to follow suit.'

'Really, you have a most unfortunate way of putting things!' complained Lady Turville.

'I study to please, dear Mama, you must know that,' he replied with a mocking bow.

'Yourself, perhaps,' put in Emmeline, tartly.

'Oh, have done, will you?' commanded their mother. 'Your Uncle Edward certainly did in one sense marry to disoblige his family, for although the bride he chose was eminently satisfactory as to fortune — indeed, no female of our acquaintance at that time was more so! — in every other way she was ineligible in the extreme. She was the daughter of a manufacturer! — a man who had worked his way up from obscure origins to become the owner of a prosperous woollen mill in Yorkshire. Naturally, we were not overjoyed at the connection. I can only think it a blessing that your grandfather Turville was not alive at the time — it would certainly have hastened his end. Of course, we had as little as possible to do with your Uncle Edward after his marriage. Fortunately, he made his home in York, and rarely came South.'

'They did visit us on one occasion, though, didn't they, Mama?' asked Emmeline, with a sudden flash of memory. 'I suppose I must have been about twelve years old at the time, so you, Frank, would have been ten, and ought to recall it, too. I remember both of us being summoned to the drawing room, and Mama and Papa were sitting there with our Uncle Edward — whom I hadn't seen for so long that I'd almost forgotten him! — and a strange lady holding a baby on her knee.'

Francis had been looking puzzled, but towards the end of this speech, he suddenly slapped his thigh, exclaiming — 'Egad, you're right, Em! Yes, I do recall it now. There was a baby — a plump, rolypoly creature. A regular Yorkshire pudding, in fact.'

He paused to give time for some expression of appreciation of this sally, but it failed to raise even the glimmer of a smile on the countenances of his family. He told himself for the umpteenth time what a dull set they were, and went on,

'Another thing I remember now is that my Uncle slipped me a guinea.'

'That's what is so unjust!' declared Emmeline. 'Why should it always be boys who are given presents of money? All I received was a box of sweetmeats!'

'Most appropriate,' remarked Francis, satirically.

'I am positive you mean something odiously unkind by that,' replied his sister, with disdain, 'so I propose to ignore it. But, Mama,' she continued, fortunately distracted by another train of thought, 'what was she like — the manufacturer's daughter, I mean? I cannot at all remember.'

'Well, I've no very clear recollection myself. After all, it was sixteen years ago, and the only occasion on which we ever met. Moreover, she and your Uncle were not here much above an hour, for it was all very awkward, you know. She was a dark young woman with a not unpleasing countenance, though lacking, naturally, in the marks of gentility. Her attire was of good quality, but not in the first fashion. One could scarcely expect otherwise, as I suppose she must have done her shopping in Yorkshire. Oh, and I do remember clearly that she had more than a hint of that unfortunate provincial accent in her voice.'

'Charming,' said Francis, mockingly. 'The daughter of this union must be altogether a delightful creature, don't you agree, Aubrey?'

'Oh, but *she* may not be so very bad,' put in Lady Turville, quickly. 'The mother died soon afterwards in childbed, and Eugenia was put in charge of someone selected by your Uncle until she was of an age to be sent to what I understand on good authority is a most select Young Ladies' Seminary in York. As a matter of fact, your Uncle did approach us to see if we would be willing to receive the child into our own family when she was made motherless,' she added. 'But on the whole, I did not think it would do.'

'Uncle Edward died some years ago, did he not?' asked Emmeline. 'So the girl is an orphan?'

Her mother frowned. 'Yes, that's the only point on which I must confess I am not altogether easy. It appears that since her father's death, Eugenia has been used to spending a considerable portion of her school holidays at the home of her maternal grandfather — the manufacturer, you understand. One cannot quite like that — there is the local accent, for one thing. However —' she brightened a little — 'no doubt we may soon put her in the way of things, once she comes among us. That is why I was particularly anxious for Lucilla to be here. At two and twenty she would have more in common with an eighteen-year-old girl than you, Emmeline. But Lucilla, of course, consults no one's convenience and interest other than her own,' she finished, in an aggrieved tone.

Emmeline Welwyn bridled. 'If you feel like that, Mama, I may as well return home! I suppose I don't need to tell you that I can ill be spared — Welwyn will scarcely know how to go on without my assistance.'

'Time he learnt, dear sister,' drawled Francis. 'Two and thirty, ain't he? And still tied to a female's apron strings.'

Emmeline's usually cold blue eyes kindled with anger. 'You always were disagreeable, Frank! How Mama can suppose that you'll have the remotest chance of fixing your interest with this girl, is more than I can imagine. You're more likely to disgust her from the outset!'

'You must know, sister,' put in Aubrey, a sneer on his somewhat discontented mouth, 'that Frank's a prodigious hit with females. One is forever hearing of his conquests in Town.'

Francis looked amused. 'You flatter me, dear boy. But of course, conversation is bound to be at a low ebb in the circles you frequent. A choice between the cut of a man's coat or his reputation, what?'

Aubrey was beginning on a retort to this taunt, when Lady Turville interrupted with a peremptory gesture. 'Enough of this nonsense! If you're to be forever brangling, you'll end by giving the girl a disgust of you both! And if anything is to come of this visit, you —' she directed a meaning glance at each brother in turn — 'must play your cards with the utmost skill. It's no matter which of you she chooses, so long as one of you marries her. And once she has left us to go to her godmother, Lady Milden, who is to bring her out into Society, you will have lost your chance, for she'll be snapped up in no time at all in Town.'

'By what you've told us, ma'am,' objected Aubrey, 'that's by no means certain. A female such as you describe certainly won't take the Town by storm! Besides, that may not be the worst of it — for all we know, she may have a squint or some such deformity, as well as being fat.'

'Mama was not describing the girl herself,' Emmeline reminded him, soothingly, 'but her mother. Depend upon it, *she* will be presentable enough. After all, she *is* a Turville.'

'Besides, however plain she may be, she won't lack for suitors,' put in Francis, cynically. 'Any girl with a fortune of that size will be a hit overnight.'

'Is it so very large?' asked Aubrey.

'My dear! Her grandfather's one of the most prosperous manufacturers in the West Riding and she is his sole heir,' explained Lady Turville.

'But there is the taint of Trade,' objected Aubrey.

'Few will care for that. Besides, as Emmeline has just said, no one can quibble at the girl's birth. She is the daughter of a gentleman, after all.'

'Well, for my part I'm not over-anxious to find myself leg-shackled,' drawled Francis, 'but one is naturally tempted when so much blunt is at stake. So which of us is it to be, dear boy?' he asked, with a mocking smile at his brother. 'Do we take it in turns on the basis of primogeniture, or shall we do the thing in more sporting style and toss for first try?'

Lady Turville had the grace to look shamefaced at this remark. 'There is no occasion to bring this affair down to the vulgar level of the boxing ring or the cockpit,' she said, severely. 'Your cousin is being sent to Town like many another girl from the provinces, so that she may get herself an eligible husband. And who, may I ask, could be more eligible than her own cousins? All I am trying to do is to put her in the way of meeting you two before all the others who are bound to come crowding round her once she is in London, and to give her an opportunity of becoming intimately acquainted with you here in the seclusion of our family home.'

'After which, if she has any sense,' remarked Francis, with a twisted smile, 'she will run screaming to the wolves in the Metropolis.'

'Well, if you don't wish to make any attempt to recommend yourself to her,' replied his mother, caustically, 'by all means stand aside and let Aubrey try what he can do. Only you have the better chance, I fancy, because you will inherit the title; and I should suppose that the girl's grandfather will require her to marry a man of rank.'

'If that's so,' said Aubrey, sounding almost relieved. 'I would appear to be wasting my time. I shall return to Town, Mama, and leave the field to your favourite.'

'You'll do no such thing!' exclaimed Emmeline. 'Any girl in her senses must prefer you to Frank — you have by far the nicer nature!'

'And he's so much better turned out, too,' said Francis mockingly, raising his quizzing glass to inspect Aubrey's tight fitting yellow pantaloons, striped waistcoat and the high shirt points which made it difficult for him to turn his head. 'What chance have I against such an elegant butterfly?'

Aubrey reddened and clenched his fists. 'B'God, for two pins, I'd — I'd —'

Francis lowered the glass, toying with it for a moment. 'You'd do what, dear boy? Draw my cork, would you say? I could almost wish I had two pins about me — can either of you ladies oblige?'

Far from obliging, the ladies did their best to throw oil on the troubled waters; at length succeeding sufficiently to bring about, if not a truce, at least an armed neutrality.

'There is no telling which of you Eugenia may prefer,' concluded Lady Turville, soothingly. 'But I think it all too probable that she may take a fancy to one of you, as she can scarcely have been in the way of meeting any young men of *ton* in Yorkshire.'

'I cannot help reflecting, ma'am, that Yorkshire may not be quite the barbarous wilderness that your fancy evidently paints it,' drawled Francis. 'I understand on good authority that the natives have quite given up painting themselves with woad, and have even been known to install Assembly Rooms in some of their principal towns.'

'Well, that's as may be,' said Lady Turville, who had not herself been any farther north than Leamington Spa, 'but I shall own myself surprised if a girl who can only just have left the schoolroom — for she is not much above eighteen — has seen anything of elegant company. That being so, it should be no very difficult task for one of you to make an agreeable impression upon her. And you must all own that it would be a great piece of folly not to make some push to keep such a handsome fortune in the family.'

For once, there was no disagreement.

Chapter II

Close to the village of Great Lydeard and only a few miles by road from Lydeard Hall stood a more recent and somewhat smaller gentleman's residence, Misbourne House. This had been built about sixty years previously as a country home by Sir Gervase Martyn, baronet, who had named it for the river which flowed nearby. Since that time, two generations of Martyns had succeeded to the property, the present owner having come into his inheritance barely two years ago. He had then been with Wellington's army in the Peninsula and, after a short furlough to attend his father's funeral, had returned there. Now, nine months after the battle of Waterloo, he had sold out of the Army and was returning home to Misbourne House.

As his travelling carriage, marked with the dust of dry country roads, turned into the drive, he looked out of the window with lively interest. He was in his middle twenties, of good height and figure, elegantly but quietly dressed in a well-fitting coat of cinnamon brown, buff pantaloons and shining Hessian boots. His fair hair curled naturally, and was cut in the prevailing Brutus style. He was not exactly handsome, but his intelligent, sensitive face was attractive in spite of its somewhat withdrawn expression, and his quiet grey eyes held a glint of humour.

The carriage drew up beside the portico of the house, and the traveller jumped down with an air of relief. But before he could mount the steps to the entrance, the door opened and a girl sped down them in a flutter of draperies and cast herself upon him with cries of delight.

'Peter — oh, Peter! Oh, how good it is to see you again!'

He enveloped the slim form in a brotherly hug. 'And you, Nell! Stop mauling my coat, m'dear, and let's have a look at you.'

He held her at arm's length, surveying quizzically the small-featured, oval face with its lively eyes and warm smile.

'So you've still got your brown locks,' he said, laughing. 'I quite thought by now they'd have turned grey, with all the fuss attendant on a wedding! And — dear me! — I do believe you're just a little plumper than you used to be.'

'Odious creature!' She wrinkled her nose at him and drew his arm through hers. 'But pray come indoors at once to Mama — she's been watching through the window for hours past, as you may well imagine! Here comes Marchant to see to your luggage, so you may leave all to him.'

An elderly manservant had followed her from the house, though in a style more befitting his years. Sir Peter Martyn stopped to exchange a word of greeting with him before being hustled indoors by Eleanor.

His mother was awaiting him in the hall. The resemblance to her son was strong, although maturity had added a sprinkling of grey to the once bright hair. She surveyed him for a moment with eyes grown suddenly misty.

'Peter!' She held him close, as if by so doing she could bridge the gulf of years between the child that had been and the man of today. She released him quickly and looked up into his face. 'You've grown thinner, my dear.'

'Oh, Mama!' Eleanor protested, laughing. 'You always say he's thinner whenever he returns after a long absence! By now, he should have quite wasted away according to your reckoning! But he actually said he thought I was plumper — isn't that detestable of him? He deserves to have Gregory call him out for it — which he very likely would do, if he were here!'

'Pooh, I take no account of a Naval man,' replied her brother, pinching her cheek. 'I suppose Meg's here with Draycott?' he asked his mother.

'Oh, to be sure, but they're out walking at present.' She lowered her voice. 'I fear they find the company a little tedious. They'll be glad to see you here. All the Aunts and Uncles are with us, of course, for the wedding.'

Sir Peter raised a startled eyebrow. 'What, including my Aunt Maria? Well, since Nelly will get married, I suppose these visitations are only to be expected. I'll go and remove my travel stains and present myself in due course.'

'Do you know, Peter, you're the only one who ever calls me Nell?' remarked Eleanor.

'And you dislike it, madam?'

She wrinkled her nose at him. 'No, only when you call me Smelly Nelly, as you did on the day when you fished me out of the village duckpond! I disliked that extremely!'

'Well, so you were — a distinctly malodorous spot, the pond at Great Lydeard. Lud, I'd almost forgotten that, myself, and you can't have been more than seven years old at the time. What a prodigious memory the girl has!'

'I recall it quite clearly. I was playing beside the pond with Meg and Lucilla Turville —' She let her voice tail away, looking at her brother with dismay clouding her expressive eyes.

'Yes, well, time for all our reminiscences later,' he said briskly, moving towards the staircase. 'I'll be getting along now.'

Eleanor waited until he had disappeared round the bend of the stairs, then turned remorsefully to her mother.

'Oh, Mama! I'd rather have bitten off my tongue!'

Lady Martyn patted her arm. 'There, my love, don't give it another thought. That affair must quite have gone by now, you know — after all, it was four years since, and he was very young, just down from Oxford. Besides he has been away fighting in Spain, with no leisure for brooding on old miseries. Depend on it, he can hear her name mentioned without a pang. Mercifully, so it is when one is young.'

But though she reassured her daughter thus, she was far from certain herself. She recalled the frank, open young man of two and twenty, with his easy yet unassuming manners which had charmed everyone; comparing that memory with her son as he was today, she was bound to acknowledge a change. The easy manners and ready wit, remained, but the openness had vanished. A reserve had set in; one could never be quite sure nowadays what he was thinking. The barriers were up even against his own family, perhaps most of all against his one-time confidante, his mother. She sighed, reflecting that perhaps it was always so when sons went from adolescence to manhood, a part of the price to be paid for one's joy in them as children. She shook off her uneasy thoughts and returned to her guests.

Sir Peter passed most of the afternoon in what he would term 'doing the civil' to his relatives, but after a few hours he had an irresistible urge to escape. He managed to catch the eye of his brother-in-law, Julian Draycott, and by common consent they edged out of the drawing room and took their way to the stables.

'Phew!' he muttered, when they had fairly made their escape. 'These family reunions are the very devil! Did you ever know anyone prose on like my Uncle Burlington, or poke, pry and meddle like Aunt Maria?'

Draycott laughed. 'Lud, yes! We've a score such in my family, assure you. But I dare say they won't stay long after the wedding, if that's any consolation. Meg and I will be returning home in a day or so, as Meg becomes uneasy if she leaves the children for long.'

They spent some time in the stables, talking to Ridge, the head groom and inspecting the horses. It was close on two years since Sir Peter had been at home, and though he had left his affairs in the competent hands of his bailiff, Mark Cooke, there were some matters which required the personal attention of the owner. One of these was the purchasing of some new animals, a topic which Ridge was quick to introduce. The head groom was obviously delighted at the prospect of having Sir Peter at home to take the proper interest which every gentleman owed to his stable; instead of leaving it to the supervision of one, who, to Ridge's way of thinking, had never fully grasped the importance of that particular department of the estate.

'There's a deal to be seen to,' remarked Peter, with a frown, as they parted from Ridge. 'I must have Cooke up tomorrow and see how matters stand with the rest of the estate — not but what he's an excellent fellow, and will have it all in good heart.'

'Settling down here, then, now that you've sold out of the Army?' asked Draycott.

'What else, my dear chap? My roving instincts satisfied, I turn to the comfort of hearth and home, what?'

'As long as they are satisfied — your roving instincts, I mean.'

'Amply, assure you. I never was one of your dashing blades, y'know, and a military life is not the ideal existence as far as I'm concerned. There's plenty for me to do here, and I've always preferred the country to Town.'

'All the same, you'll go up to London now and then, I suppose?'

Sir Peter's expression closed up. 'Might do — can't say.'

Draycott judged that he had asked enough questions about his host's future plans, and switched easily on to less personal topics. They had been strolling idly along the drive leading from the stables to a side gate, which they now reached. Sir Peter consulted his watch. He was reluctant to return to the house yet, and saw that there was still time before dinner to walk on towards the village of Great Lydeard, which lay at the end of the lane, about half a mile distant.

They set out accordingly, and had covered half the distance when a horseman approached them raising a cloud of dust.

'Faugh!' exclaimed Peter, with a grimace. 'Must the damn fellow gallop?'

But evidently there was no fault in the rider's manners, for on seeing the pedestrians he slowed his horse to a walking pace and the dust subsided. As he drew level with them, he let out a yell of recognition.

'Peter Martyn, b'God!'

He swung out of the saddle, gathered the reins in one hand and offered the other to Peter.

'How are you? Home for y'sister's wedding, I suppose? Devil of a time since we last ran across each other — four years, somethin' like that?'

Peter took the outstretched hand and agreed that it was indeed so long since they had last met.

'Dare say you remember Meg's husband, Julian Draycott,' he concluded, indicating his brother-in-law. 'You were at their wedding, I recall.'

The two men bowed to each other.

'Thing is, he may not remember me,' said the other, with a chuckle. 'Never very clear-headed at weddings, are we, especially one's own! Francis Turville, at your service. My family and the Martyns used to run wild together as children — recall Meg, of course. How does she do?'

Draycott was able to assure him that Margaret was in the best of health, and for some time the three stood chatting on commonplace topics.

'Not walking down to the village, by any chance?' asked Frank Turville, presently. 'If, so, perhaps you'd care to look in at the house? Must warn you, though, m'sister Emmie's there, not to speak of my younger brother Aubrey. Not but what it's worth a visit, only to see how Aubrey's togged himself up since he's been shaking a loose leg in Town — fine as fivepence, give you m'word!'

Sir Peter declined courteously, but suggested that they might instead all three adjourn to the Lydeard Arms, a comfortable hostelry which stood in the village quite close to the pond. This met with general approval, and before long all three gentlemen were standing with tankards in their hands in the tap room of the inn.

The Lydeard Arms was a Tudor building with its tap and coffee rooms divided only by a low portion of dark oak in which was set an opening so that patrons might pass easily from one room to the other. As the tap room was at present empty, the three gentlemen assumed that they had the place to themselves, so did not trouble to moderate their voices as they talked.

'And what brings you home, Frank?' asked Sir Peter. 'As I recall, you were never a frequent visitor to Lydeard Hall.'

Francis took a long pull at his ale. 'Oh, some damnable scheme of m'mother's. She's forgetting me hitched up to a

Yorkshire cousin of ours — rather, I should say, for one of us, either Aubrey or myself. It makes no matter which, the girl's free to choose.'

Sir Peter laughed. 'I must say you sound like an eager suitor! I'd no notion you had any cousins in Yorkshire.'

'Dare say you might not — bit of a skeleton in the family cupboard. Father's younger brother married some millowner's daughter. Did well for himself in one way — pots of money, y'know. This girl's their only child, and since they're both dead, she'll inherit all the old man's wealth. M'mother thought we might as well make a push to keep it in the family.'

'I see.' There was no humour now in Sir Peter's eyes. 'And do you suppose the young lady herself will prove amenable?'

'God knows, dear boy. Never met her but once, and then she was only a babe. Regular Yorkshire pudding, by what I remember.' Francis brought out his former jest, thinking it too good to waste on one performance. 'But she's to go to London later to be brought out by some female or other — her godmother, I think — so Mama, with her usual forethought, hit upon the bright notion of bringing Aubrey and myself home to have a touch at her before she's thrown on to the Marriage Mart.'

'So you've no notion what manner of female she may be?' asked Draycott, with raised eyebrows. 'A bit of a gamble, eh?'

'Oh, my expectations are not great,' replied Francis, carelessly. 'After all, what can one expect from the wilds of Yorkshire, as my respected parent so wisely points out? A rough accent, no doubt, perhaps manners to match; what will all that signify beside the indisputable charms of a large fortune?'

'What indeed?' echoed Sir Peter, drily. 'Your circumstances must have changed for the worse, Frank, since we last met, if you are hanging out for a wealthy bride.'

'My pockets ain't precisely to let, if that's your meaning, Peter. But one can never have too much blunt, after all, so I'm prepared to swallow my well-known objections to matrimony in pursuit of so worthy a quarry. I mean of course, the fortune not the female,' he added.

'So it's to be war to the knife between you and Aubrey? Or do you have a gentleman's agreement to take it in turns to woo the lady?'

'Well, I did offer to toss him for first try,' admitted Francis, with a laugh. 'But that brought m'mother down on me like a load of coals — you know how females like to wrap everything up in clean linen. So the field's open, and devil help the hindmost — tally ho!'

His ringing call caused two ladies seated unseen behind the partition in the coffee room to jump violently. They had been sitting rigidly upright in their chairs up to that moment, having reluctantly been obliged to overhear every word of the foregoing conversation.

The older of the two turned an indignant look on her companion. 'Well, I must say, Miss Ginny!' she exclaimed in a furious undertone. 'I've a good mind to go and give them something to think about!'

She half rose from her seat, but the lady beside her, who was quite young, hastily pulled her back.

'Stay where you are, Nancy!' she commanded in a fierce whisper. 'Leave this to me — I'll show them, see if I don't!'

Chapter III

Francis had only just returned home after his meeting with Sir Peter when the somewhat ramshackle carriage kept for hire by the landlord of the Lydeard Arms drew up outside the house, depositing two ladies and a quantity of baggage on the doorstep.

On being informed that the visitors were none other than Miss Eugenia Turville and her abigail, the butler, though well trained, showed surprise. He quickly recovered, however, and civilly requesting the abigail to be seated in the hall, conducted the young lady to a parlour where Lady Turville was sitting with her daughter, Mrs. Welwyn.

Both started to their feet when the visitor was announced, and for one brief moment stood surveying her without speaking. Their first feeling was one of relief. Eugenia Turville was neither dowdy nor plump, and even the most searching scrutiny failed to reveal any disfigurements such as the squint which Aubrey had unkindly supposed. The young lady was of medium height with a slender but shapely figure; dark brown curls clustered about a face which had a pleasing line from brow to small, firm chin, and from which a pair of intelligent hazel eyes gazed back at her hostess. She was becomingly and fashionably attired in a dark blue merino pelisse trimmed with fur and a bonnet of the same colour with white, curling feathers. Lady Turville took a deep breath and moved forward to welcome her niece.

'Eugenia, my dear child! We were not expecting you to arrive today, or one of your cousins would have come down to the village to meet you. I am so sorry you were obliged to find your own way.'

'Eh, don't put yourself in a taking, ma'am.' Lady Turville flinched at the broad Yorkshire accent, and drew back quickly from the peck which she had just bestowed on her guest's cheek. 'I've a tongue in my head, so I reckon I can ask my way as well as the next. We had to wait on the landlord's chaise, though, as it was already out on hire when we arrived.'

'Oh — oh, indeed, what a pity,' murmured Lady Turville, casting a despairing glance at her daughter. 'By the way, this is your cousin Emmeline, Mrs. Welwyn. I do so hope you will be friends.'

'There's nowt against it that I can see,' replied the disconcerting young lady, as she shook hands.

'No — er — very true,' floundered Lady Turville. 'Well — er — Emmeline will take you up to your room, my dear, for you must be longing to wash off the dust of your journey. I will give orders for your maid to be sent up, and the luggage.'

After Emmeline had conducted their guest from the room, Lady Turville collapsed in a chair for a few moments to calm her natural agitation. Then she summoned a servant to request Mr. Francis and Mr. Aubrey to come to her immediately. They appeared almost simultaneously, as both happened to be indoors.

'What's all the to-do, Mother?' asked Aubrey, petulantly. 'I was about to decide on my evening wear, and now I've had to leave Orchard in suspense, not knowing what to lay out. Pray make haste and let me go, or there will scarce be time to present a creditable appearance at dinner.'

Francis consulted the clock with a sardonic eye. 'Don't worry, dear boy. If you had two or three hours in which to dress instead of only one you would contrive to look just the same — insufferably dandified. A pity to waste so much effort on your own family, don't you think?'

Lady Turville drummed her heels on the carpet. 'If you two don't stop bickering, I declare I shall have a spasm! It is too much!'

They both looked at her in some surprise, for she was a strong minded woman not usually given to hysterical outbursts.

'What the devil's amiss, ma'am?' demanded Francis, contracting his heavy dark eyebrows.

'Everything!' Lady Turville's tone was dramatic.

'Nothing wrong with Father, is there?' asked Aubrey, cautiously.

'No, no — this is nothing to do with your father! It's your cousin Eugenia —'

'The Yorkshire pudding?' asked Francis, with a grin. 'What about her? Had she decided not to pay us a visit after all?'

'On the contrary,' replied his mother, struggling to regain control of her feelings, 'she is already here — she arrived only a few moments since, and Emmeline has taken her upstairs!'

'Well, all's quite satisfactory, then,' said Aubrey, with relief. 'And now I can go and change my dress. Even you —' turning to his brother with a malicious look — 'will want to spend rather more time than usual on that office, now there's to be company.'

'It is far from satisfactory!' exclaimed Lady Turville, tragically. 'Only wait until you meet your cousin!'

Aubrey looked taken aback, and Francis whistled.

'Very bad, is she?' he asked.

Lady Turville flung out her hands in a gesture of despair. 'Impossible! Quite impossible!'

'Impossible, eh? Fat as a bladder of lard, I collect?' asked Francis, with a comical look of dismay.

His mother shook her head, unable to say any more for the present.

'Squints, then?' persisted Francis. 'B'God, Aubrey, you guessed aright, it seems —'

'No, no! It is far worse than that!'

'*Worse?*' Francis stared. 'Squints in *both* eyes, what?'

His mother shook her head again.

'Pock marked face?' suggested Aubrey.

'Wooden leg?' put in Francis, at the same moment.

'No, no — I almost think it's worse, in a way —' stuttered Lady Turville, weakly.

'Well, damned if I can think of anything worse than all that!' declared Francis, at last. Then, suddenly struck by a new idea, he asked — 'I say, ma'am, she ain't a *dwarf*, by any chance, is she?'

Lady Turville recovered her full voice. 'No, but she might almost as well be! Oh, she's presentable enough in appearance, and dresses with taste, which is more than one could reasonably have hoped for! But her *voice* —' he own broke on the word — 'oh, dear, as soon as she so much as opens her mouth —'

'— she puts her foot in it, does she?' finished Francis, grinning broadly. 'Well, there had to be something y'know, Mother. Stands to reason, don't it, with all that fortune?'

'It might not have been so bad,' conceded Lady Turville dejectedly, 'if she had possessed only the same degree of that hideous accent as I noticed in her mother. But the daughter's is very much broader — and, worse than all, she makes free use of the vulgar idiom, besides! Only imagine, when I said that I hoped she and Emmeline might be friends, she replied "that there was *nowt* against it that she could see." I thought I should sink through the floor — every feeling was outraged to hear such an expression on the lips of a gentlewoman!'

'Nowt?' repeated Aubrey, in a puzzled tone.

'Nothing, clodpole,' prompted his brother. 'Consider the context. Well, I for one shall be surprised if she keeps to that opinion after a better acquaintance with our dear sister.'

'And is that all you can say?' demanded his mother, with a heightened colour. 'Upon my word, Francis, I have often suspected that your unfortunate levity tended to obscure your sense, but I never saw a more convincing example of it than now!'

'Well, as Frank appears to consider it all such a good jest,' remarked Aubrey, disdainfully, 'he can have the heiress to himself, for I beg leave to withdraw. I refuse to be burdened with any wife who would lessen my credit in the *ton*, be she never so wealthy.'

'Whereas I, dear boy,' drawled Francis, 'shall count on my credit to survive introducing any bride of my choice, even if she were the veriest Gorgon. But pray don't let us come between you and your valet Orchard in the all-important matter of the tasteful arrangement of your neckcloth. Even if you've quite given up the motion of captivating the Yorkshire Pudding, you will still wish to preserve your reputation for dazzling the rest of us.'

But later, when Francis actually set eyes on his cousin Eugenia, he realised that the amusing soubriquet he had bestowed on her definitely would not do. Her figure, in the stylish white muslin evening gown embroidered round the hem with pink roses, was such that even a connoisseur of his large experience could not fault. His eyes rested appreciatively on it for several moments before moving to its owner's undeniably attractive countenance.

But her voice, which in spite of his mother's warning caused Aubrey to start violently when first he heard it, was altogether another matter. On being informed by the vision in white muslin that she was 'reet glad' to make his acquaintance, Francis, however, rallied nobly and made a graceful bow.

'And I, too, am — er — reet glad, Cousin,' he answered, smiling in his most winning style. 'May I have the honour of taking you in to dinner?'

A family dinner at Lydeard Hall was never a comfortable occasion, but on this particular evening the atmosphere was more strained than usual. Lord Turville, an easy-going man in his fifties who allowed himself to be managed by his wife, had never much conversation to offer on any but sporting topics. Having greeted his niece cordially and asked her if she could ride, he would have considered his duty in that direction done; but he found that his civil enquiry not only produced from Eugenia an enthusiastic assent, but served to unleash on the surprised assembly a flood of equestrienne reminiscence. As this was delivered in homely Yorkshire idiom, a good deal of it was unintelligible to most of her audience. As far as their understanding went, however, much of the discourse seemed to concern a number of unladylike exploits with a character called Tom, who appeared to stand very high in Miss Eugenia Turville's estimation. Alarmed for the prosperity of her scheme, which nevertheless seemed hourly less attractive, Lady Turville ventured to ask if Tom was a relative.

'Nay,' replied Eugenia, airily, 'he's nobbut my groom, but he's a reet gradely lad, that he is!'

Francis had been watching her closely for some time, fascinated in spite of himself by the lively, changing expressions which flitted across her face. Detecting a spark of mischief in her hazel eyes, he began to gain the impression that she was enjoying some private jest. He laughed softly, and led her on to entertain them further on the same subject.

But this would not do for his mother, who felt that Eugenia had been allowed to expose herself quite enough for one evening. In a smooth but determined way, she contrived to draw her niece into a discussion with herself and Emmeline on the latest feminine modes. Eugenia proved quite as ready to talk volubly on this fresh topic as on the first. What she had to say showed no lack of interest or taste; the voice in which she said it, however, continued to assault both ladies' ears. The gentlemen of the party experienced some relief when at last the ladies left them to the welcome solace of a glass of port.

'Phew!' ejaculated Aubrey. 'Mother is quite right. She's an impossible female — wish you joy of her, Frank.'

'Oh, I don't know,' said his father, tolerantly, as he filled his glass from the decanter. 'Pretty little thing, ain't she, and looks the lady. Probably shy, y'know, — hard on anyone to be plumped down among a set of strangers. Wonder how she came by that devilish ugly mode of speech, though?'

'Simple enough, sir, I should have thought,' replied Francis. 'Taking on the colour of her environment, surely?'

Lord Turville pursed his lips. 'Well, that's just it, m'boy. My brother Ned took some queer notions into his head now and then, but I'll lay any odds he'd never have permitted a filly of his to talk in that style. What's more, your mother swears to it the chit attended one of these devilish high-starched girls' seminaries in York — quite the crack, by her account. Should have thought they'd have beaten it out of her there.'

'I hardly think, sir,' objected Aubrey, 'that they beat female pupils.'

'More's the pity — do some of 'em good. There were no such scruples in my day. But things may be different now, with all these namby-pamby notions going about. What with poor relief for farmworkers sending the rates sky-high, and other such lunacy, the country's going to the dogs, if you ask me. Which reminds me — there's to be a meet at the Lydeard Arms the day after tomorrow. You'll come, of course, Frank. What about you, Aubrey?'

'I beg you'll excuse me, sir. You may have forgotten that I never hunt.'

'Dammit, boy, I quite thought you'd have come round to a more normal way of life by now,' said his father, with a rare touch of irritation. 'However, as you wish. You'll come, Frank?'

Francis hesitated. 'Something depends on what plans my mother has for Cousin Eugenia.'

'Eh? You'll never let a chit stand between you and a good day's sport?' asked Lord Turville, incredulously. 'Oh, well —' suddenly recollecting his wife's instructions — 'I suppose you must do what you can in that direction.' He brightened suddenly. 'Tell you what, why not bring her along, too? The gal says she's fond of riding, and Em likes to come out. They won't come beyond the second field, I dare say, like most of the other females, but it will enable you to join us. Better for them than moping about indoors with a damned piece of embroidery, too, or whatever else it is females find to do. Yes, a capital notion, what?'

Francis agreed that this plan might answer very well, and the party adjourned to the drawing room. They found Lady Turville looking somewhat exhausted, while Emmeline was gamely endeavouring to hold her own in a conversation with the ebullient Eugenia. After the tea tray had been brought in, Lady Turville, with considerable presence of mind, suggested that their guest might be glad of an early night after her long journey. She was greatly relieved when Eugenia agreed to this and retired, leaving the rest of the family to a welcome cessation of hospitality. For lack of any more congenial employment, Francis and Aubrey took themselves off for a game of billiards, leaving Lord Turville alone with his wife and obliged to lend a reluctant ear to her complaints.

'Well!' she began. 'I hope we are not fated to endure many more evenings of the kind! Upon my word, I had no notion that the girl would prove so difficult! She never stops talking, you know, and in that dreadful voice which I find past all bearing! I tell you, Turville, I begin to wonder whether I have not made the grossest error in ever thinking of her for one of our sons, fortune or no!'

'As to that,' he relied, equably, 'I don't myself set much store on either of 'em marrying an heiress. Damme, Sophia, they're plump enough in the pocket already not to make it an object.'

'But Francis is expensive, as you very well know. Besides, it seemed a pity to let all that money go out of the family. Or at least, it did,' she added, despondently. 'Now I'm not at all sure, if it means accepting a girl like that.'

'There's little amiss with the child,' said her husband, soothingly. 'She's decorative enough, at all events.'

'But that voice!'

Lord Turville considered. 'It's quite a sweet ton y'know, Sophia, underneath that ugly brogue. Tell you what, I dare say she'll lose it when she's been with you and Em for a few weeks. After all, she's young enough to learn, ain't she? And females are good at that kind of thing — adaptable. Yes, depend on it, that's how it will be.'

Meanwhile in the seclusion of her bedchamber Eugenia seized her maid Nancy about the waist and whirled her round the room in a transport of high spirits.

'Oh, Nan!' she exclaimed. 'Such fun — you'd never believe!'

'Have done, do, Miss Ginny!' Nancy, who had been in Eugenia's household since that young lady's birth, tried to make her tone severe. 'By the look on your face, I reckon you've been up to some of your tricks. What is it this time?'

Eugenia released the abigail and flung herself down on the bed, gurgling with laughter.

'Their faces!' she gasped. 'They thought me odious — and so I was! If I know anything, they'd be positively *glad* to see me go tomorrow! Didn't I tell you I'd find a way to deal with them?'

Chapter IV

A burst of spring sunshine enlivened the scene outside the Lydeard Arms on the morning of the meet. It added lustre to the glossy coated thoroughbreds and the hunting pink of their riders assembled on the village green, from which the geese had fled hissing in disapproval. From the door of the adjacent smithy, the blacksmith peered out, hammer in hand, to watch the assembled riders moving to and fro, and the inn servants coming out with foaming tankards for those who had journeyed some distance. Every now and then, another gig would rattle across the courtyard of the inn and its occupant hastily jump down to claim his mount from a waiting groom.

Presently Sir Peter Martyn arrived with his sister Margaret and her husband. They looked about them, then Margaret leaned sideways in the saddle to drop a confidential word to her menfolk.

'That girl standing over there with the Turvilles — she must be their young cousin from Yorkshire, I think. A pretty child, don't you agree?'

Their glance followed hers to where Eugenia, looking very much at her ease, was sitting a jaunty black mare with a white blaze on its forehead. It did not escape their notice that she was wearing a modish olive green riding habit and matching hat with a plume of curled feathers.

'By Jove!' exclaimed Julian Draycott, approvingly. 'Francis Turville was faint and far off, what, Peter? Not much of the Yorkshire pudding there, and that outfit looks all the crack, too.'

'Yorkshire pudding?' asked Meg, puzzled.

Sir Peter laughed softly. 'A jest of Turville's — not worth repeating. But I fancy the young lady must have come as a surprise to her — ah — affectionate relatives.'

Meg saw that there was a story here, and determined to have it from her husband later. For the moment, she was obliged to hold her peace while they all exchanged greetings with old friends and neighbours. Presently the Turvilles moved over in their direction, and they were introduced to Eugenia. Before more than a few words had been exchanged, however, the arrival of the hounds diverted the attention of Lord Turville and Francis. They moved away; and Emmeline having been caught up in conversation with another lady nearby, Eugenia was left for a moment standing with Sir Peter Martyn's party.

'Do you hunt much in Yorkshire, Miss Turville?' Meg asked, by way of conversation.

Eugenia shook her head. 'I don't really hunt at all, ma'am, not truly, that is. Occasionally I go out with the others just for the riding, but I always turn back before matters become too serious. You see—' she lowered her voice, and looked about her in a pretence of timorousness — 'although I mustn't allow anyone else to hear me say such a thing in this company, I'm really on the side of the fox. There! I dare say I've shocked you prodigiously.'

She smiled in what both the gentlemen privately found a captivating way, although it was obviously unstudied. They laughed, and Meg gave an answering smile.

'On the contrary,' said Sir Peter. 'But one quite appreciates that such sentiments must considerably mar your enjoyment of a meet.'

She considered him for a moment with a frank, open look from her intelligent hazel eyes. Like her astute manufacturing grandfather, she had a trick of making swift appraisals of people. She decided that she liked what she saw; a quiet gentleman, less forceful perhaps than her cousin Francis, but with sufficient strength of character behind the seeming gentle indolence.

'Are you to make a long stay in this part of the country?' continued Meg.

'My Aunt has invited me to remain with her for a month, until I am engaged to go to my godmother Lady Milden in London. But as to that —' Eugenia stopped and gave a little shrug. 'I am not perfectly certain,' she finished, lamely. 'The arrangement is not definite.'

'Well, at any rate, you will be with Lady Turville for a little longer. I know that my mother, Lady Martyn, would be happy to see you accompany your relatives to my sister Eleanor's wedding. It is to be next Wednesday. May we have the pleasure of sending you an invitation?'

Eugenia made a graceful bow. 'Thank you — I shall be honoured, ma'am. Is your sister here with you today?'

Meg laughed. 'With her wedding only five days' time? No, Miss Turville, you must surely realise that she has scarce a moment to herself, what with fittings and other such important feminine matters!'

'Truth to tell,' put in Julian Draycott, 'we ourselves really came out today to escape from all that, eh Peter?'

Sir Peter nodded, but said nothing, content to watch the changing expressions flitting over Miss Eugenia Turville's mobile face. He began to think that Frank Turville was a lucky dog.

Francis returned to his cousin's side at that moment, apologising for having been obliged to leave her.

'Nay, no need to fratch yoursen,' replied Eugenia, as she nodded to the others and moved away beside him. 'I've done well enough on m'own think on.'

The Draycotts and Sir Peter stared after her.

'Well, I'm damned!' exclaimed Julian. 'Did you hear that? Some kind of jest between them, I suppose.'

Meg began to laugh. 'Oh, yes, it must be, of course! But doesn't she do it well? I would never have believed it was the same girl speaking, would you?'

'No,' agreed her brother, thoughtfully. 'No, certainly I would not.'

'They're moving off,' remarked Julian.

A toot of the Huntsman's horn had started the hounds on the business of the day, and they all trotted off along the lane which led to the coverts, the group on the village green following in procession. Eugenia was now riding beside Emmeline, with her cousin and uncle slightly ahead of them at some distance from the Martyns. To reach the covert, they had to cross a tussocky field through which the Misbourne flowed. Eugenia noticed that the pollard willows lining the stream were flaunting catkins, and within the wood bunched primroses revealed yellow tips. She reflected that Spring came earlier in the milder air of this southern country, and felt a sudden unaccountable exhilaration of spirits as if at the prospect of some delight in store.

The riders made their way slowly along the main ride of the wood, while some little way ahead the Huntsman could be heard cheering on the hounds among the trees and undergrowth. Emmeline seemed to be having some trouble with her horse, an elderly roan mare which was unaccountably reluctant to respond to its rider's intentions.

'I don't know what can be the matter with Jenny,' she said irritably. 'I've ridden her often enough in the past.'

'Did you say, Ginny?' asked Eugenia, with a laugh. 'That's what I'm called at home — short for Eugenia, you know.'

'Indeed,' replied Emmeline, in a quelling tone. 'Well, we shall not call you so here. But I actually said JENNY —' she spelt it out. 'I dare say you may find as much difficulty,' she went on, condescendingly, 'in understanding my manner of speech, as we do in comprehending yours. We must have a little talk together on that subject at some time, but now is not a suitable moment.'

'Happen it isn't,' replied Eugenia, at her most Yorkshire. 'And th'canst spare th'breath for t'future, too, think on.'

Emmeline was about to make an indignant if dignified reply; but at that moment a shrill hulloa came from the far side of the wood and the riders began to gallop after the sound. Francis and Lord Turville, caught up in the excitement of the chase, soon outdistanced their womenfolk as they followed the leading riders out of the wood to race across an adjoining field, clods of earth being thrown up by flying hoofs as they went.

The ladies followed among a huddle of other riders until they came to a low hedge separating the first field from the next. Without pausing, Eugenia set her mare at the hedge and sailed easily over; but Emmeline was not so fortunate. Although the hedge was well within the scope of both Jenny and her by no means inexpert rider, for some reason they fumbled the jump.

Hearing a cry behind her, Eugenia reined in sharply and turning, saw Emmeline lying on the ground and the riderless Jenny galloping away. With an exclamation of dismay, she slipped from her horse and ran to her cousin's side.

Several other riders had looked round on hearing Emmeline's cry, among them Sir Peter Martyn's party, who had been just a little way ahead. All three wheeled their horses to return to the aid of the two ladies, Julian Draycott grasping the bridle of Eugenia's mare as he passed.

'Here, look after Merlin, will you, Meg?' said Sir Peter, jumping down from his horse. 'Let's see if she's badly hurt.'

He joined Eugenia, who was bending over her cousin. It was evident that Emmeline had not suffered enough injury to deprive her of the power of speech. She was holding forth with great vehemence on the black-hearted Jenny's conduct.

'Never mind all that,' said Eugenia, brusquely. 'Where have you hurt yourself — is anything broken, do you think?'

'I'm as right as a trivet!' replied Emmeline, crossly. 'Don't think it's the first time I've taken a toss — I'm winded, that's all. If you'll be good enough to assist me rise, Peter, I'll do well enough.'

On hearing this speech, some later arrivals on the scene who had paused for a few moments to see if any more help was needed, decided to press on after the rest of the hunt. Sir Peter obediently raised Emmeline from the ground and set her on her feet. She at once let out a yelp of pain, leaning heavily against him.

'My ankle!'

He lowered her to the ground again. 'With your permission, I'll take a look at it. I'm not without experience in these matters.'

Emmeline nodded. She had paled slightly and she gritted her teeth as Eugenia, in response to a gesture from Sir Peter, very carefully removed her cousin's half boot so that he could examine the injured ankle.

'No bones broken, I think,' he said, after a few moments. 'I'd say it was a sprain, but your medical man will tell you for certain.' He stood up, looking about him. 'What happened to your horse? We can lead you back on her to the inn and then find a conveyance to take you home.'

'The wretched brute ran off!' exploded Emmeline, whose nerves were naturally a trifle overset, although she was an indomitable woman. 'And what's more, I refuse to mount her again, even if someone is to lead her!'

'That's all right,' said Eugenia, soothingly. 'You shall ride my mare, and I'll lead her. There's no occasion for us to trouble Sir Peter Martyn and his relatives any further. That is,' she added, glancing at Sir Peter, 'if he will be so obliging as to assist you to mount.'

But Sir Peter was firm in insisting that he had no intention of leaving the ladies to make their own way home, a point of view which was warmly seconded by Meg. It was soon settled that Emmeline should be conveyed to the inn on Meg's placid mare, with Sir Peter leading the animal and Eugenia walking beside it in case — though Emmeline scoffed at this — the sufferer should suddenly feel any inclination to swoon.

In spite of this brave front, it was clear that Emmeline was feeling some pain from her accident, for she scarcely uttered a syllable during their return journey to the inn. Meg, riding Eugenia's mare, had gone on ahead with her husband, who also had charge of Sir Peter's horse, to commandeer a vehicle for their use. Eugenia and Sir Peter had little to say to each other beyond matters pertaining to the comfort of their charge; but by the time they at last reached the inn, Eugenia felt that in some curious way she had reached a stage of friendship with her companion which years of ordinary social intercourse might not have achieved.

For his part, he had taken a quiet pleasure in glancing back from time to time at the slim figure walking beside the mare; in studying the curve of her cheek as she turned to speak to

Emmeline, or the way in which her dark brown curls stirred in the light breeze. She had apologised in the beginning for keeping him from the hunt, but in truth he found it no penance to be walking with her instead.

When they arrived at the inn, they found Meg and Julian Draycott waiting for them with the landlord's hire carriage. The three ladies were installed in this for the short journey to Lydeard Hall, Sir Peter and Draycott accompanying them on horseback.

Characteristically, Lady Turville made no fuss about her daughter's accident, seeming more put out than concerned. Sir Peter and his relatives civilly declined her invitation to stay for some refreshment, and promptly took themselves off, expressing the hope that Emmeline would soon be feeling better.

'Of all the tiresome starts!' exclaimed Lady Turville, when they had gone. 'One would think, Emmeline, that you were a sufficiently accomplished horsewoman not to take a toss at the first fence you come to! If it had been Eugenia, now, one might understand it!'

'Not all Yorkshire lasses are cow-handed, ma'am, think on!' Eugenia retorted, with deliberate intention to shock.

'*Eugenia!*' Lady Turville turned a horrified look on her niece. 'That such a vulgar expression should *ever* pass the lips of a female of breeding —'

'Ay, but I'm not, am I? Leastways, not by your reckoning,' returned Eugenia, accusingly.

'You are a Turville,' stated her Aunt, coldly. 'It's an ancient line, and the name must convey distinction on whomsoever bears it. If you have picked up an — er — unfortunate — trick of speech from living too long in the North, that does not alter the fact that you are a young lady of Quality. And I have strong hopes that we may soon see some improvement in your diction, now that you are removed from undesirable influences.'

Eugenia's chin went up.

'I'm also an Ackroyd, think on, and let me tell you, ma'am, it's summat I'm proud on! So if by undesirable influences you mean my dear Granpa —'

Eugenia had been only half in earnest, but now she was genuinely aroused. Her Aunt realised that she must retract a little if she wished to avoid alienating the girl completely, a drastic step to which so far she had not quite reconciled herself, although she was wavering.

'By no means,' she replied, in a propitiatory tone. 'Far be it from me to interfere with your very natural affections.'

She turned to her daughter, who had been paying little heed to the conversation, but was lying in a dejected attitude on the sofa where she had been placed.

'I think perhaps you will be better off lying down on your bed for a few hours, Emmeline. The doctor will be here presently to tell us the extent of your injury; but even if it should prove to be no more than a sprained ankle, you are bound to have suffered a shock, and should have rest and quiet.'

As Emmeline made no objections to this suggestion, it was plain to anyone who knew her intrepid nature that she was feeling somewhat shaken. She was accordingly helped upstairs by two of the footmen and put to bed by her maid.

When Francis and his father returned to the house several hours later, they were surprised to hear of Emmeline's mishap.

'Em must be losing her touch,' said Francis, incredulously. 'Even Aubrey could manage Jenny.'

But when he and his father went round to the stables, where they found the miscreant Jenny safely returned, they solved the mystery of the animal's unusual behaviour. It seemed that a tendon in one of her legs had been giving some trouble, but none of the grooms had thought to mention that fact when she was led out for Emmeline to ride. Lord Turville made his displeasure felt, and Emmeline's reputation as a horsewoman was cleared.

Chapter V

Emmeline declined to come downstairs to dinner that evening, having a tray sent up to her bedchamber instead.

'Poor Em! That's not like her,' commented Lord Turville, as the family gathered round the table. 'Always full of pluck, what?'

'Well, she is approaching thirty, after all,' said his wife, 'And she has brought four children into the world.'

'Damme, Mother, Em's as strong as a horse,' objected Francis. 'Not one to take to her bed for a sprained ankle.'

'It may be,' replied his mother drily, 'that she realised the conversation this evening would be confined to a relation of the events of today's hunt.'

The remark was not unjustified, for already her husband and elder son were deep in reminiscence. Aubrey sat silently by, until asked by Lady Turville how he had passed his day. He gave a guilty start, and mumbled that he had done nothing much.

'Nothing all day!' she repeated. 'You must have occupied yourself in some way — where did you go?'

It was to escape questions such as this that both her sons had decided to leave the paternal roof as soon as possible. Aubrey wriggled uncomfortably and said he had been out in his curricle over Wendover way.

'And what can you have found to do there, pray?'

It was at this point that Eugenia took pity on a plight which she could easily recognise, and launched forth into one of the near-monologues with which she had attempted to enliven the family conversation during the past two evenings. This time her theme was her grandfather's manufactory; and she spared her unwilling auditors no detail concerning processes of which they would much rather have remained ignorant, and people whom they could feel relieved never to have any prospect of meeting. The only alleviation of their sufferings was that they had the usual difficulty in following much of what she said.

Francis listened to her with amusement during the brief intervals when he was not exchanging hunting talk with his father, now and then prompting her to continue by asking a question, much to his mother's annoyance.

As the ladies rose from the table at the end of the meal, Eugenia suggested that they might perhaps look in on Emmeline to see if she felt in need of company.

'Happen I might read to her,' she offered helpfully.

Aubrey bit back an exclamation, and his mother made a noise suspiciously like choking, but Francis nodded with an encouraging smile.

'A capital idea, Cousin Eugenia! We will all come, once we have finished our wine.'

'Have you no consideration for your sister's nerves?' asked Lady Turville, thinking more of her own. 'She needs rest and quiet, not a roomful of chattering people about her.'

'You know best, of course, Mother,' replied Francis; then added with malicious enjoyment, 'But there's no need for the rest of us to forego the pleasure of hearing Eugenia read aloud. We must find a suitable book presently.'

Eugenia's eyes, sparkling with fun, met his for a moment before she turned to leave the dining room with her sorely tried Aunt. He looked after her consideringly. Could she possibly be as ingenuous as she seemed?

Lady Turville did go up to visit her daughter, but she managed to persuade Eugenia to let her go alone. She found

Emmeline sitting on a chair with her leg supported on a footstool, placidly working at some embroidery.

'So you are feeling better,' she said.

'Right as a trivet,' agreed Emmeline, putting her work aside, 'apart from the pain of this odious ankle, that is.'

'Would you care to join us in the drawing room for a while?'

Emmeline made a face. 'If my cousin's as talkative as usual, no, thank you. It was largely to escape her conversation that I decided to remain up here during dinner! I felt quite myself again a few hours after the doctor left, as why should I not? I hope I'm not such a poor creature as to make an invalid of myself over a toss from a horse and a trifling injury.'

'You were very wise, for I never knew anyone rattle on as that girl does — and in that odious voice! You'll never believe,' continued her mother, with a shudder, 'what topic she selected for her conversation this evening! She talked of nothing but her grandfather's manufacturing concerns — as though she could possibly suppose that we would wish to know anything about trade, or those who engage in it!'

'Dreadful!' agreed Emmeline. 'Mama, what are we to do about her? You cannot still think it a good notion to wed her to either of my brothers? I very much fear that even with her fortune she could never be acceptable in Polite Society.'

'I am rapidly coming round to that opinion myself,' said her mother, gloomily. 'It is all very well for your father to say that she will learn to model her speech on ours when she has been with us a little longer! My own feeling is that it would take years, not merely weeks, to effect such a change. And even then, there would remain this fatal propensity for talking away nineteen to the dozen — so improper in a young female, at any time! And on such subjects too! I tell you, Emmeline, I have retired to bed with the headache every night since she arrived, and hardly know how I can bear any more of it!'

Emmeline nodded absently, for she had been thinking about something her mother had said earlier.

'Do you know, Mama, I wonder if Papa could be right? About Eugenia's manner of speech, I mean. I wasn't feeling at all the thing this morning when the Martyns brought me home, so I didn't pay much heed to what was going on around me; but it did seem to me —' she wrinkled her brow in an effort at recollection — 'that she not only behaved with more propriety towards them than she shows to us, but that her voice was much improved, too.'

'I dare say you may have imagined it,' objected her mother, sceptically. 'After all, you had just suffered a shock to your system.'

Emmeline agreed reluctantly that this might be so. 'Well, what is to be done?' she continued. 'I suppose you can scarcely turn her out of the house before the time settled for her to go, as any such slight offered to her would surely be resented by her godmother? And I understand Lady Milden is a person of some consequence in London, so it wouldn't do for her to take a grudge against our family.'

'No, indeed. I fear we must make the best of it,' said Lady Turville, despondently. 'Francis and Aubrey must take her out driving or riding for most of the day if the weather holds, then perhaps she will be too tired to talk during the evening. And I've decided to write again to Lucilla and see if I can persuade her to come. Now that you'll be unable to get about for a while, Eugenia will have no female companion on her outings other than myself — and I really feel,' she added, with a heartfelt sigh, 'that I am too old for the responsibility. In truth, I never felt my age before as I have done since your cousin arrived. This is what comes of trying to do one's best for one's family. Be warned by my example, Emmeline, and never allow yourself to become a martyr to yours!'

'I doubt if you'll persuade Lucilla to come,' answered Emmeline, ignoring the self-pitying part of this speech.

'I'm not so sure.' For the first time, Lady Turville brightened. 'I intend to mention that Peter Martyn is at home.'

'You think she's still interested in that quarter?' asked Emmeline, dubiously.

Her mother shrugged. 'Well, she may have other notions now, but four years ago she was ready enough to receive his addresses. In fact, it took quite some persuasion —' she flushed, and went on hastily, 'but, of course, you know all that. Ah, well, if I cannot induce you to join me in keeping your cousin entertained this evening, I suppose I'd better return to the drawing room. The men will be there presently, and then perhaps we may get up a game of cards — but five is such an awkward number. Still, perhaps I could sit out and do my needlework — yes, that will be the thing to do. Anything, so that we may have a little respite from the girl's obnoxious voice!'

Chapter VI

Emmeline was downstairs to breakfast on the following morning, managing to move around with the aid of a stick, and seeming otherwise no worse for her accident. When the meal was over, Eugenia said she had some letters to write. Her Aunt thankfully saw her settled in a corner of the library, then returned to sit in the morning room with Emmeline. Aubrey disappeared on some mysterious errand of his own, while Francis accompanied his father out of doors to attend to the business of the estate.

An hour or so passed by in a quiet tranquillity which Lady Turville had definitely decided she could never again hope to enjoy while her niece remained under her roof. Presently the butler announced some callers, and Sir Peter Martyn walked into the room with his sister Meg. Lady Turville was not surprised to see them, for neighbourly civility required that they should call to enquire after Emmeline; but she would have been more at ease if her menfolk had been present. Sir Peter had not been inside Lydeard Hall for four years, and the disagreeable memory of his last visit had still not entirely faded.

This was probably why she summoned Eugenia to the morning room, trusting to her niece's customary volubility to cover any awkward pauses there might be in the conversation. But for once Eugenia was a disappointment in that direction; having greeted the visitors, she sat silently listening to the somewhat constrained efforts made by the others. After a while, Meg turned to her, holding out a card.

'I've brought your invitation to my sister's wedding, Miss Turville. My mother wishes me to say how very pleased she will be to see you there should you be at liberty to attend.'

Eugenia accepted the card, cast a look almost of desperation in her Aunt's direction, and mumbled some words of thanks. In spite of the low, hurried tone of her voice, there was no mistaking its strong Yorkshire accent.

Meg stared, momentarily disconcerted, and Sir Peter raised a quizzical eyebrow.

'You're not very gracious child,' chided Lady Turville, privately wondering what could be amiss with one usually only too ready to burst into speech. 'It is prodigiously good of Lady Martyn to include you among her guests at such short notice.'

'Oh, yes,' said Eugenia, hurriedly. 'I am indeed sensible of Lady Martyn's kindness.'

Meg made a polite rejoinder, and very soon afterwards the couple rose to leave. When they had gone, Lady Turville also went from the room, leaving Emmeline and Eugenia together.

'Well!' remarked the former. 'You had precious little to say for yourself, Cousin! Had the cat got your tongue, as my old Nurse used to say?'

'Come to that,' retorted Eugenia, with spirit, 'seemed to me t'cat had been busy all round!'

'Well, yes,' admitted her cousin. 'It was an awkward visit, but it was only to be expected that they would call to ask how I did — common civility, you know.'

Eugenia nodded, drawing her black brows down in a frown. 'Why awkward?' she asked, bluntly. 'Haven't you known each other all your lives?'

'Oh, to be sure. My parents and the Martyns were never *intimate* friends, but being such near neighbours, they naturally saw a great deal of each other. And the children of both families often played together — Frank and Peter, who were much of an age, were especially friendly during their schooldays. Later on, Eleanor Martyn — she's the one who's getting married, you know — shared a governess for a time with my sister, Lucilla, whom, so far you haven't met. But that was all before —'

She broke off, and Eugenia looked a question.

'I dare say you may as well know, for there's no doubt that sometimes ignorance of such matters may lead to an embarrassing situation; and you must not be offended, Eugenia, if I tell you that you are not always the soul of tact.'

'Nay, you can't offend me,' promised Eugenia, blithely. 'But do go on, Cousin.'

'It was during that time I just mentioned, when Lucilla and Eleanor were sharing a governess, that Peter Martyn began to take notice of my younger sister. She was fifteen then, and he was three years older. She was — still is — a prodigiously lovely girl,' said Emmeline, loyally swallowing the childhood jealousy of her sister's beauty which she had never completely overcome. 'She had that extremely blonde hair, with blue eyes and almost perfect features, and a figure to match. Even at that age, all the local young men were attracted to her; and later, when she had her come-out, all the Town beaux were at her feet. However, she remained here in the country until she was close on eighteen; and during all that time, she and Peter were meeting, whenever he was down from Oxford. He was very much in love, and she — well, you've met him and can see for yourself what a personable young man he is, so you can imagine that she wouldn't be completely indifferent to him. In the end, he applied to my father for her hand just before she was to go up to London for her come-out.'

'Reckon he refused, then, since they didn't marry,' Eugenia stated.

'Not quite that. My parents said Lucy was too young and inexperienced to be thinking of marriage before she had seen anything of Polite Society; but that if she and Peter were of the same mind when she returned home after her London season, they would consent to the match. The thing was, of course,' explained Emmeline, 'that Mama felt Lucy could do a deal better for herself than marry Peter Martyn. His fortune even in those days was handsome, owing to a legacy from a great uncle; but his expectations otherwise were not large, for he was heir to a smaller estate than our own and a mere baronetcy. Mama had set her heart on a peer for Lucy, and she was not to be disappointed. Once in Town, Lucy was besieged by eligible admirers, and she succeeded in capturing the biggest matrimonial prize of them all, the Earl of Ruscombe.'

'Do you mean she fell in love with him?'

Emmeline laughed. 'Lud, Cousin, you're very ingenuous! But at your age all a girl thinks of is falling in love, I suppose. The Earl was close on seventy and she was just eighteen, so you may judge for yourself. Lucy was widowed two years after the marriage, and now at two and twenty she is left with everything a female could desire in the way of title, position and fortune. Everything except children, that is,' she added, thinking fondly of her own brood at home. 'For my part, I think nothing of a childless marriage; and I wouldn't change places with my sister for all her fine house, carriages and servants, and going to all the *ton* parties!'

Eugenia nodded. 'Ay, you're reet there — I'm of the same mind, mysen.'

'Yes, well, I'll allow that your notions on some points may be very proper,' conceded Emmeline, 'but I do wish you could

cultivate more elegance of speech. It is past all bearing at times
— can you not try?'

'Happen I will. But tell me how Sir Peter Martyn took the
news?'

'Oh, very badly! He came down from his final year at Oxford
to find that all was settled and Lucilla was betrothed to the Earl
of Ruscombe. As he couldn't believe that she had fallen in love
with Ruscombe — well, who could? — he appealed to her to
cry off the engagement. When she stood firm, he rounded on
Mama and accused her of putting ambition before her
daughter's happiness. There was quite a scene, and Mama
declared he should never enter the house again! But Papa, who
never opposes my mother in anything as a rule, said that he felt
for Peter and gave it as his opinion that the boy had been
shabbily used.'

'Ay, poor lad,' Eugenia put in, softly.

'Well, and perhaps he's not so much to be pitied! *He* thought
that Lucy was being coerced by Mama into the match, and that
all the time she was still attached to him. But I can tell you that
it was no such thing,' declared Emmeline, emphatically.
'Perhaps I shouldn't speak so of my own sister, but if ever
Lucy had any feelings for anyone but herself, I've never seen it!
She knew very well what she was about and did her utmost to
bring on Ruscombe's addresses! However, Peter was quite cut
up over the affair, and shortly afterwards joined Wellington's
Army in the Peninsula. He sold out after the battle of
Waterloo, and has not long been back home at Misbourne
House. He's master there now, as his father died a few years
back. Frank says he means to settle into the life of a country
gentleman, so I suppose my parents can expect to be seeing
him frequently in future. But the first meeting was bound to be
a little awkward for Mama, as you'll readily understand.'

'I do that.' Eugenia rose. 'If you'll excuse me, I'll finish my letters.'

She returned to the library. No one else had arrived to disturb her peace, so she sat down again at the writing table, taking up her pen. For some time it remained poised unused above the paper, while she thought over what she had just heard.

It seemed that her Aunt had always been of the same mind, not scrupling to scheme for her family's material advancement regardless of their true happiness. The luckless Lucilla had been persuaded into a match with a rich nobleman old enough to be her grandfather; and now her two brothers were being set on to try and catch a wealthy mill-owner's granddaughter as a bride. For Lucilla there might be some excuse, Eugenia thought. On whom should a girl depend for advice in such matters, if not on her mother? Eugenia herself had never known a mother's care. The vacant place had been filled by others, kind and loving, yet not perhaps with quite the same influence. Or it might be that she was more self-reliant than the general run of females of her age. However it was, she felt convinced that she would have put up the strongest opposition to exchanging Sir Peter Martyn for some doddering greybeard, had the latter been a Prince of the Blood.

Yes, even though one might make allowances for her cousin Lucilla — for Emmeline's insistence that Lucilla herself had desired the match with Ruscombe could be discounted as springing from the jealousy of a plain sister for a beautiful one — there was no valid excuse for Francis and Aubrey. They were full grown men and should think shame to permit their mother to dictate their actions. It was obvious that they were cast in the same mould as Aunt Sophia, and allowed greed to overcome every scruple.

Her usually gentle expression hardened. Well, she fancied they had met their match! Forewarned was forearmed; and once she had learnt what kind of girl they expected their cousin from Yorkshire to be, she had done her utmost not to upset their preconceived notions. It was famous fun, too! Perhaps a little exhausting at times, but well worth the effort. Even at this early stage of her visit, it was clear that her Aunt, at any rate, was beginning to have second thoughts about her suitability as a wife for one of her cousins. So much the better! In a short time — perhaps a few days, perhaps a little longer — she would be able to curtail her visit without any regrets on either side. Godmama would be delighted to see her in London earlier than she was expected, so that could be soon arranged.

Her face changed, softening suddenly. There was one small regret, she acknowledged to herself. It was a pity that she had been forced to sustain her part in front of Sir Peter and his pleasant sister. *There* she would have preferred to appear to advantage. However, it could not be helped; it was a part of the tangled web that always resulted from deception.

She sighed. Did he still think of his lost love, she wondered? Emmeline had admitted, if reluctantly, that her envied young sister was a prodigious beauty. Could Eugenia Turville possibly hope to compete with such a one?

'A blonde, not a brunette like me.' She was unconscious of having spoken the words out loud. 'No, most certainly not anything like me.'

She started violently as a voice spoke from behind her.

'Who isn't anything like you, Cousin?'

She turned to see that Aubrey had entered the room quietly and now stood looking down at her with a puzzled expression on his face. A little colour came into her cheeks.

'Eh, I was just talking to mysen, lad! Pay no heed.'

'Seems to me,' he remarked, looking at her closely, 'you ought to do more talking to yourself, Cousin Eugenia. It has a beneficial effect upon your voice.'

She turned away, hastily scribbling a few words at random on the paper before her, to cover her embarrassment. 'Go away, Cousin — can't you see I'm busy?'

'I beg your pardon for intruding, Eugenia, but I have something very particular to ask you, and this seemed a chance to see you alone.'

Chapter VII

Eugenia dropped her pen, making a blot upon what had already become a wasted page, and turned to face him with dismay in her eyes.

'Something very particular?' she repeated.

'Yes,' replied Aubrey, absently. Then realising all at once the trend of her thoughts, he exclaimed in horror — 'Good God, no! Not what you're thinking — at least, I collect you are — not anything like that, assure you! No, it was simply that I wondered if I could prevail on you to drive out with me this afternoon. Without Frank, you know — just the two of us, in my curricle.'

She stared at him without speaking for a moment.

'Why?' she asked bluntly.

'Why?' repeated Aubrey, foolishly. 'Well — er, well — I thought you would like to see something of the countryside. M'mother suggested —'

'But why without your brother?'

'Dash it, Eugenia, you must know you can't get three in a curricle! Besides, I can go on very well without Frank's company at any time.'

'Happen *you* may,' said Eugenia, drily. 'But will *we*, think on?'

'Will we —?' He stared at her in puzzlement for a moment, then his face cleared. 'Oh, if you're wondering if it would be proper for you to come out with me alone —'

'Nay,' she interrupted him, 'I reckon there's nowt wrong socially with being escorted by my cousin, or my Aunt would soon inform me of it! I may as well speak plain,' she went on, giving him a challenging look. 'If you mean to get me on my own so's you can make up to me, don't put yoursen about!'

'Well!' exclaimed Aubrey, in disgust. 'I must say, Eugenia — and you can dashed well tell Mother that I'm uncivil if you like! — I never came across a female with less delicacy of mind than you!'

'And I never came across a lad with less spirit than you!'

'Indeed, madam!' he retorted, in some heat. 'Then allow me to tell you that, even disregarding that abominable accent of yours, there is nothing about you that could possibly induce me to make up to you — as you so vulgarly put it! There! You aren't the only one who can speak plain!'

She applauded quietly, a mocking light in her hazel eyes.

'Oh, well done, Cousin! I didn't think you had it in you to fight back. Well, since you don't want to get me alone for the usual reason, what *is* your reason?'

He looked taken aback. 'It's as I said at first. Naturally, we always take guests for outings around the countryside, and since Emmeline is laid up for the present, the duty falls to Frank and myself. M'mother does not care overmuch for driving or riding,' he added.

She laughed suddenly. 'You're gammoning me, Aubrey, but that's no matter. Yes, I'll come.'

He thanked her with what she thought excessive gratitude, then left her to complete her interrupted task.

Over a cold luncheon, Francis also invited her out for a drive and seemed quite disconcerted to learn that his younger brother had made the application before him.

'Changed your mind, eh!' he asked Aubrey, cryptically. 'Very well, I shall know how to deal with you. Perhaps you will do me the honour, Cousin Eugenia —' with a little bow in her direction, 'to permit me to drive you into Aylesbury, the day after tomorrow? As tomorrow is Sunday, I suppose —' with a cynical look at his mother — 'driving, except to church, will be barred.'

'I am relieved to see you display so much proper feeling,' said Lady Turville, drily.

She did not know whether to be pleased or vexed when Eugenia signified her willingness to fall in with this scheme. It would certainly be an unqualified blessing to be relieved of the girl's company as often and for as long as possible. It was gratifying, too, that her sons should pay so much heed to her instructions. On the other hand, the last thing she desired now was for either of them to fix his interest with Eugenia. She must lose no time in acquainting them with her change of course, and meanwhile hope that Lucilla would condescend to come in response to her appeal. Lucilla could then take over what Lady Turville could only think of as the arduous duty of entertaining their tiresome guest for the duration of her visit, while Francis and Aubrey would be free to return to Town if they chose. No doubt they would; she had never flattered herself that Lydeard Hall held any attractions for either of them nowadays.

Eugenia came downstairs later dressed in a modish cherry red pelisse lavishly trimmed with fur and an entrancing velvet bonnet of the same colour. Lady Turville thought sadly how perfectly her plans would have turned out, had her niece's social endowment matched her physical ones. She sighed as she watched from the window Aubrey helping Eugenia up into the curricle and placing a rug round her, then she turned away to what she hoped would be a relaxing afternoon in her daughter's company.

Aubrey was not such a celebrated whip as his elder brother, but he could manage his curricle efficiently enough for

Eugenia, never a nervous passenger, to be able to enjoy the drive. The day was exceptionally warm for March and the exhilaration of Spring was in the air. Birds swooped here and there searching for food and nesting material, new born lambs bleated in the meadows, even the grass took on a fresher green.

'And now,' said Eugenia, when they had turned out of the drive into the lane which led to Great Lydeard, 'you can tell me the real reason why you wished me to come out with you.'

Aubrey's hands faltered on the reins for a second, causing the horses, a prime pair of chestnuts, to swerve slightly. He corrected them quickly.

'The real reason?' he repeated, with more than his usual slight lisp. 'Don't be absurd, Cousin — I told you.'

'You told me nowt that I could believe!'

At that moment, they drove over a small bridge spanning the river. 'That's as you choose,' he replied, hastily. Then, with the appearance of one imparting valuable information — 'This river's the Misbourne, by the way.'

'Oh, ay?' Eugenia invested the Yorkshire phrase with all its cynicism.

'Yes — they do say that when the Misbourne changes its course, it presages a national disaster. But as it's done so several times without anything remarkable occurring that I ever heard of, perhaps we shouldn't refine too much on the saying.'

'Happen we shouldn't,' she agreed, giving him an amused glance. 'Where are you taking me?'

'I thought you might care to visit Wendover,' he said, with an attempt at a careless tone. 'It's a fine old town. And afterwards if you'd like to walk a little, we might leave the curricle at the Red Lion and go part of the way along the track that leads to Bacombe Hill. That won't be too dirty with all the dry weather we've been having recently; but I don't suggest we climb the hill today, though there's a splendid view from the top. The summer's the best time for going up there, unless one wants to wade through mud.'

Eugenia expressed agreement with his plan, and settled back in her seat to enjoy the fine bursts of country which presented themselves on either side of the highway on which they were now travelling. They passed several other vehicles, including a number of farm wagons, and were held up once by a herd of cows crossing from one field to another; but otherwise they reached Wendover almost an hour later without incident and with very little further conversation between them.

Aubrey drove into the yard of the Red Lion, helped Eugenia down, and gave his equipage into the hands of a waiting ostler. Having offered her some refreshment, which was refused, he then took her on a tour of the town. As it was only small, this was soon completed; and eventually he guided her along a lane on the outskirts which led to the track he had mentioned.

Eugenia had noticed that ever since their arrival in Wendover, Aubrey had been constantly pulling out his watch to study it. She wondered what lay behind his obsession with the time, but a question on this point only brought an evasive reply and a quick flush to her cousin's cheek. She did not press for an answer, confident that she would eventually elucidate the small mystery for herself.

They had walked a short distance along the lane without meeting anyone before they came to the track leading up the hill; but almost as soon as they had turned into it, two riders approached from the opposite direction. One was a young lady of about Eugenia's age, the other a groom. The riders halted on seeing the walkers, and the groom respectfully held back a short distance. Aubrey stepped quickly to the young lady's side, removing his hat. She bowed, blushing prettily, and said, rather breathlessly, 'Oh, Mr. Turville! Fancy meeting you!'

Yes, fancy, thought Eugenia with an amused look at the flustered young face. She was a pretty child, fair and fragile looking, with enormous, innocent blue eyes.

'Yes, by Jove, quite a coincidence, what?' replied Aubrey, glibly. He turned to Eugenia. 'Allow me to present my cousin to you, Miss Mandeville. Miss Eugenia Turville, who is staying with my parents for a while.'

Eugenia and Miss Mandeville exchanged greetings, then both fell silent, each studying the other.

'We were about to walk a little way towards the hill,' explained Aubrey. 'That is, if it's not too dirty farther up?'

'Oh, no, it is not at all bad until one reaches the second bend, is it, Clinton?'

The groom agreed gravely, still keeping his distance.

'I suppose —' Aubrey hesitated, looking at Miss Mandeville in a manner which reminded Eugenia of a lost dog — 'you wouldn't care to leave your horse in Clinton's charge, and take a stroll with us for ten minutes or so, — that is, if you're quite sure it won't be too dirty underfoot for you?'

'Oh, no!' replied Miss Mandeville, hastily. Then, looking quite shocked in case he might have misunderstood — 'Oh, yes — I mean, yes I would like to come, and no, I'm sure it isn't in the least bit dirty underfoot!'

The groom, who behaved throughout as one acting in a well rehearsed play, jumped down from his horse and assisted his mistress to alight before Aubrey could perform this office himself. He then led both horses on to some grass at the side of the track, apparently prepared to await Miss Mandeville's pleasure.

'I think, you know,' remarked Eugenia suddenly, 'I won't come with you, if you don't mind. I'll stay and keep your groom company.'

They both protested politely against this; Aubrey in particular saying that the walk had been intended for her benefit, and if she felt too tired then they would not go any farther.

'Nonsense!' exclaimed Eugenia, firmly. 'I'll come to no harm here, and two's company, when all's said.'

Miss Mandeville blushed again at this remark; but Aubrey, deciding to take Eugenia at her word, placed the young lady's arm in his, saying that they would return in ten minutes or so.

Eugenia watched them go with a tolerant, amused eye, then turned to find very much the same expression on Clinton's face. At once she began an easy, casual conversation with the groom, chiefly concerning the various points of the two horses in his present charge.

'I can see you understand horses, Miss,' he remarked, admiringly.

'Well, yes, I do. My father was a keen huntsman and kept a good stable, and I learned to ride from my earliest years.'

This led on to a discussion of the merits of different breeds, and the ten minutes had lengthened into twenty without either Eugenia or the groom finding the waiting too tedious. At this point, they saw Aubrey and Miss Mandeville coming slowly towards them, evidently absorbed in each other.

At once, Aubrey began to apologise to Eugenia for keeping her waiting, but she brushed this aside, saying she had not noticed the time.

'I think we should be getting back now, though,' he said, reluctantly. 'Once the sun goes, you'll find it cold in the curricle, Cousin.'

'It's a deal colder where I come from,' she answered, with a shrug. 'But happen we'd best go.'

They said their goodbyes, Aubrey lingering over the slender gloved hand which Miss Mandeville placed in his. Then, giving Eugenia his arm and with many a backward glance until the riders were lost to view, he escorted her back to the inn.

'So that was your reason for coming this way, today,' she said, with a teasing glance. 'But why bring me? You'd have done well enough on your own.'

He made no answer for a while, then burst out — 'If I come out alone, m'mother's so devilish set on asking where I'm going. She's never lost the trick, even though I've lived in Town now for close on three years — as if I'm some dashed scrubby schoolboy still! There's no bearing it!'

She nodded sympathetically.

'I say, Eugenia,' he continued, encouraged by her expression, 'can I ask you a favour?'

'That depends,' she replied, cautiously. 'But try me.'

'Well, it's just that — well I'd as lief Mother didn't know,' he said, haltingly, 'that I met Miss Mandeville this afternoon.'

'Is Lady Turville acquainted with her?'

'Slightly. One knows everyone in the country, y'know — everyone of consequence, that's to say.'

'And Miss Mandeville's family is?'

'Eh? Oh, see what you mean. Yes, they're Quality, right enough, live in an old Manor house just outside Wendover.'

'But?'

'What d'you mean, but?' he repeated.

'There must be a but,' said Eugenia, bluntly, 'or you and t'lass wouldn't need all this havey cavey business.'

He made no reply to this, and they covered the rest of the way to the Red Lion in silence. Once there, the curricle was brought out and they started on the road back to Lydeard Hall.

After they had been driving along for some time without speaking, he gave an awkward little cough which caused Eugenia to look up at him. There was a smile in her eyes which emboldened him to speak.

'I say, Eugenia,' he began, awkwardly, 'can I trust you not to blab to Mother? You haven't answered me yet.'

'What do you take me for?' she answered, scornfully. 'I'm no tale-bearer!'

'Well, a fellow's not to know,' he said, defensively. 'And females are prodigious blabsters, say what you like, forever running home with some tale or other!'

'I shan't let t'cat out of t'bag.' Her tone was decided.

He cast a grateful look at her. 'You're a right one, Eugenia! I'll do you a favour some day, see if I don't.'

'You can do me one now — call me Ginny. I'm always called so at home, and I miss hearing it, except from my maid Nancy.'

'Very well, Ginny it is. And since I feel I can trust you, Ginny, I'll tell you all about Hetty — Miss Mandeville, I mean.'

Eugenia nodded, settling herself down more snugly under the sheepskin rug, for the air was cooler now.

'As I said, we've had a slight acquaintance with the family all our lives — Sir John Mandeville is a Justice, rides to hounds with m'father, that kind of thing. I was at school with one of Hetty's brothers. He asked me over there when I was spending last Christmas at home. I'd never seen Hetty before, not to notice, y'know. She'd been away at some seminary or other, but she was back at home. Well, you saw her.' He looked at

Eugenia challengingly. 'Wouldn't you say she's just about the most stunning girl you ever set eyes on?'

'She's certainly very pretty,' agreed Ginny, with a twinkle in her eye.

'Yes, well, I know a fellow should never praise one female to another, but I think you're too dashed straightforward for that kind of flummery! Don't mind admitting to you, Eugenia — Ginny — I was fairly bowled over.' His face clouded over, and he shook his head. 'Knew it was no good, though. Could never come to anything.'

'Why on earth shouldn't it?'

'She's no fortune, y'see. Good family, but too many of 'em. Three girls younger than Hetty and three boys, with my friend Walter the eldest.'

'What does that signify?' asked Ginny, impatiently. 'You've some money of own, haven't you? Enough to marry on, surely?'

'Depends how you look at it,' he answered glumly. 'I've an independence, and m'father makes me an allowance besides. Together, that would be enough, certainly. But —'

'But unless you marry with your parents' approval, the allowance would stop?' cut in Ginny quickly.

'Exactly. You've hit on it at once. And I know that Mother's expectations for me — er — go beyond Miss Mandeville,' he finished, awkwardly, with a side glance at his companion.

'Oh, aye.' She produced the telling phrase once again. 'Happen you're not the only one who knows that. Well, Aubrey, since you've been good enough to tell me your secret, I'll tell you one of mine in exchange. But you must promise to keep it quiet.'

'Word of a Turville!' he assured her.

Chapter VIII

Apart from a visit to the parish church of Great Lydeard, Sunday passed uneventfully away. After the service several of their neighbours paused to chat awhile with the Turvilles; and Ginny was perforce presented to them, if reluctantly, by her Aunt. To that lady's great relief, her niece contented herself with acknowledging the introductions by a smiling bow and a greeting so low as to be barely audible. This behaviour, so different from anything she had anticipated, brought the surprised Lady Turville more than one compliment to the effect that Miss Eugenia was a very pretty-behaved and attractive young lady.

'So different from some of these modern misses!' pronounced one old lady with a back like a ramrod and notions to match. 'Always putting themselves forward at the least opportunity, and with positively no respect for their elders! Anyone can see, Lady Turville, that your niece has been well brought up.'

Lady Turville thanked the speaker for these sentiments with what she hoped the other would not notice was a sickly smile; and quickly moved Ginny on, before the wretched girl could do anything to shatter the favourable impression she had so far made.

Sir Peter Martyn had also been present in church, accompanied by enough relatives to fill several pews besides the family one. Ginny had glanced once or twice at the tall, upright figure, until on one occasion their eyes chanced to meet, when she had looked hastily away; but not before she had caught his quick smile. He spoke to her afterwards in the churchyard, briefly presenting her to his mother and his younger sister, Eleanor, who was soon to be married. Lady Martyn bestowed a warm smile on her neighbour's visitor, and said how glad she was that Miss Turville would be attending Eleanor's wedding ceremony, for an acceptance to the invitation had been sent to Misbourne House the day before. Ginny liked her on sight, and felt equally drawn to her daughter Eleanor; but she was unable to do more than reply with the barest civilities, since she was surrounded by so many others, including her Aunt and Uncle. She parted from the Martyns with feelings of regret that she told herself impatiently were out of all proportion to the degree of acquaintance.

A stroll about the grounds with Francis and Aubrey for company provided some cynical entertainment for the afternoon. Each was constantly striving to score off the other, while Francis insisted on treating her with extravagant gallantry until she laughed him out of it.

'You'll do nowt by that road,' she informed him with her usual bluntness. 'I'm not one of your bits of muslin, think on!'

'No, really, Ginny, I say,' protested Aubrey. 'Ought not to talk like that — dashed improper for a female.'

Frank's dark eyebrows shot up. 'Ginny, is it? You two seem to have come to an understanding yesterday.'

'Happen we did — though not in the way you mean,' countered Ginny.

'Ah, but how do you know what I mean?'

'Because she dashed well realises that anything you say must mean something unpleasant,' put in Aubrey, quickly.

'Dear boy, I don't think our cousin requires you to interpret between us,' drawled Francis.

'Oh, have done, do!' exclaimed Ginny. 'You should've outgrown those nursery tricks by now! Let's go back to t'house — Emmeline needs company, poor lass.'

'I wonder?' murmured Francis.

Far from taking offence at this, Ginny laughed wholeheartedly, and recommended him to save his sarcasm for those who could understand it, and not waste it on a simple Yorkshire lass.

'A Yorkshire lass you undoubtedly are,' he replied, smiling down into her dancing eyes, 'but simple — ah, there I beg leave to differ.'

They returned to the house, where Ginny kept Emmeline company until it was time to change for dinner. The older woman was agreeably surprised to find that for once her young cousin felt no desire to batter her about the head with talk, but instead passed the time in sharing some recent copies of the Ladies' Magazine and making shrewd comments on the fashions displayed there.

But during and after dinner, Eugenia regrettably returned to her usual form. Lady Turville, driven to desperate measures by the fact that it was Sunday and therefore cards were quite out of the question, hit upon the bright idea of suggesting some music. Her sons' reception of this was no more than lukewarm, but Lord Turville was fond of a musical evening round his own fireside now and then, and he himself settled Eugenia at the piano. She asked what they would like her to play.

'Anything,' said Lady Turville, then added hastily — 'That is to say, anything you wish, my dear niece.'

Ginny gave her a mischievous look, then her expression changed as she sat for a moment, fingers poised over the keys, considering what to choose. Francis stood close by, watching her. There was something almost seductive, he thought, in the line of her profile from brow to chin and the arch of her slender neck as she at last raised her head. She struck a few introductory chords, and began to sing in a low, musical tone.

'A North Country maid up to London had strayed,

Although with her nature it did not agree...'

The song was not unknown to her hearers, and the gentlemen, at any rate, listened with appreciation.

'No doubt did I please I could marry with ease,

Where maidens are fair, many lovers will come,

But he whom I wed must be North Country bred

And carry me back to my North Country home.'

She signalled to them to join in the chorus, Francis and his father obeyed with gusto, Aubrey more self-consciously, while the ladies remained silent. After this she was encouraged to play some other songs in which the whole company could take part.

'Pray don't ask me,' protested Lady Turville. 'I have no voice — not the least in the world, I assure you, but I am very happy to listen.'

But everyone else joined in, and the ensuing hour was one of the most agreeable the younger Turvilles could remember passing at home for many years. As for their mother, she was quite content with any arrangement which prevented Eugenia from exercising her considerable talent for unending conversation.

When the tea tray was brought in, Francis came to sit by Ginny.

'Are we to take it, Cousin,' he asked, with a quizzical look in his eye, 'that you chose your song with the intention of conveying a message?'

'You mean the first one I sang?'

He nodded.

'You must think what you like,' she replied, shrugging.

He bowed. 'I am grateful for the permission. In that case, I think that possibly you did. I wonder, now, have you some north country bred gentleman in mind already?'

A little colour came into her cheeks. 'Nay,' she answered, shaking her head. 'I was nobbut homesick for a moment.'

He tried to pursue the subject, but she shook him off; moving over to sit beside her Aunt, whom she proceeded to weary with an animated account of the successive stages of her musical education from infancy to the present day, delivered as usual with a wealth of Yorkshire idiom. Lady Turville was grateful for Emmeline's occasional attempts to interrupt her cousin's monologue, but nothing could stem the flow of Eugenia's eloquence for long. Looking about her distractedly for relief, she saw that Francis and his father were deep in a sporting conversation, as usual; and that Aubrey was regarding his cousin with a curious look on his face. She tried to interpret his expression, but Eugenia would not give her leisure to pursue the matter. As usual, she was glad to take herself off to bed, reflecting thankfully that yet one more day had passed away towards her ultimate release from as trying a guest as she had ever known.

Chapter IX

Ginny awoke early the next morning and looked out of the window on another bright day.

'I'm going for a walk, Nancy,' she announced, on a sudden impulse.

'Not before you've had your breakfast, I hope,' replied Nancy, disapprovingly.

'Yes, why not? The others will still be abed, and I'll be able to have a little time on my own. You can't know what a treat that will be!'

'Well, wrap up warm and don't go too far,' Nancy cautioned her. 'And try if you can keep out of mischief for once, do.'

Ginny promised dutifully enough, but as Nancy watched her retreating form down the drive some twenty minutes later, the abigail remained sceptical. Too resty by half, the girl was; it would be a good thing when they left this place and went to Lady Mildren's, where Ginny would feel really welcome. Nancy shook her head. She could not altogether approve of the dance Miss Ginny was leading her present hosts, but then who could blame the child, after all?

Ginny turned out of the gates in the direction of Great Lydeard, head raised as she sniffed the air appreciatively. The hedges were bursting into green, and here and there against the banks on either side of the lane she caught a glimpse of purple among the clusters of violet leaves. A sparrow flew across her path, dropping a minute twig which had been intended for nest building. The bird paused, fluttered, and was gone; there were plenty more twigs to replace that one.

Her thoughts wandered to yesterday's meeting with the Martyns. In her mind's eye she saw again Sir Peter's broad shoulders as he stood in the family pew at church, and the warmth of his smile as he turned and caught sight of her. Something in the remembrance of that smile caused once more the sudden lift of spirits which she had felt on the day of the hunt. Was this what they meant by falling in love, she wondered? But it would not do for her to fall in love with Sir Peter Martyn, it would not do at all. It was unlikely that their paths would ever cross again once she had quitted Lydeard Hall; and even if she delayed going until the time originally agreed upon, that still left only a few weeks in which to improve their acquaintance. Besides, she thought ruefully, she had loaded the dice against herself. Instead of being able to appear before him to advantage, she was forced to adopt the hoydenish pose which she had assumed to pay out her Aunt and cousins for their heartless scheming. She sighed. No doubt all happened for the best, as Nancy never tired of telling her. Perhaps Sir Peter still clung to the memory of his lost love; and now that the beautiful Lucilla was a widow, there was nothing to stand in the way of a reconciliation between the two. Hateful creature! she thought bitterly; then kicked at a stone in her path with such force that she hurt her toe. The momentary pain quenched her anger. She smiled at herself, thinking she had become a hoyden in all reality. Whatever would Grampa Ackroyd have to say to her, if he knew? He was so proud of the fact that his granddaughter was a lady, and could take her place alongside any female of Quality in the land. Dear Granpa! Her face softened as she thought of the rugged old man who had struggled from obscurity to wealth, aided only by an astute mind and unremitting industry, and whose proudest moment had been when his only daughter married into the Quality. He had stood in considerable awe of his high born son-in-law, whom he had never quite been able to understand, although the two seldom clashed openly. He had deferred to the Hon. Edward Turville's wishes in a totally uncharacteristic way, until it came to the matter of Eugenia's education, where he stood firm against the girl continuing with a governess.

'Nobbut the best schooling for the lass,' he declared, firmly. 'There's grander schools now nor when we sent her mother off to learn gentry ways and talk, and our little Ginny shall have t'pick o't'bunch.'

And so she had, Eugenia reflected, remembering lessons in deportment and other social graces besides learning of a more academic kind. She had made several enduring friendships with well born young ladies whom she hoped to meet again later on, when she went to stay with Lady Milden in London. But all this had never taught her to look down on her grandfather, or to lose the warm affection she would always feel for the county of her origin and its plain, uncompromising turn of speech.

She was so deep in her own thoughts that she reached the village almost unaware. She paused on the green and idly watched the ducks moving smoothly over the pond, now and then waggling their tails in the air as they reached for some underwater delicacy. There seemed no one about at present. The door of the Lydeard Arms stood open, but there was no movement on the cobbled forecourt.

After a while, she heard footsteps approaching from behind her, and turned to see who was coming this way. It was a small boy in homespun breeches and a grubby shirt, clutching in his arms a piece of sacking securely tied with cord. As he drew nearer, Ginny saw that the bundle in his arms seemed to be invested with a life of its own, for it heaved and squirmed so violently that the child had great difficulty in retaining his hold on it. At almost the same moment, she realised that a series of mewings and spittings were coming from the bundle.

'What have you got there?' she asked the boy sharply.

He was too occupied in keeping a firm hold on his bundle to attempt any reply to the question, so she repeated it more loudly.

'Cat, Miss,' he said, somewhat short of breath, and walked past her to the edge of the pond.

'A *cat*!' repeated Ginny. 'And what in the world are you going to do with it?'

'Drownd it, Miss,' he gasped.

'That you're not!' exclaimed Ginny, aghast. 'You can't drown a full-grown cat, you cruel monster, you!'

'Watch me!' he shouted defiantly, as gathering all his strength, he flung the bundle into the pond.

Without a moment's pause for thought, Ginny lifted her skirts and plunged into the pond after it. The outraged ducks fled quacking on to the bank as she groped about in the water, trying to retrieve the bundle before it sank to the bottom. After several attempts, she managed to grab hold of it at last but she was promptly rewarded by a frantic set of claws which had managed to penetrate the sacking and now fastened themselves in her wrist. She let out a shout of pain and almost dropped the bundle again. In her efforts to retain her hold upon it, she stumbled and fell full length in the water.

'What the devil —?'

She heard the shout while she was still floundering about, trying to regain her footing on the slippery base of the pond. A moment later, she felt herself being seized about the waist and dropped bodily to the bank, still holding desperately on to the bundle.

She looked up momentarily into the puzzled face bending over her as she crouched there, panting, dishevelled and soaked to the skin.

Her rescuer was Sir Peter Martyn.

'It's a cat!' she gasped, setting the sodden bundle down on the ground and trying with numbed, wet fingers to undo the knots which secured it. 'That odious boy was trying to drown it — oh, pray help me! It's stopped struggling and it's mewing pitifully — I do hope I'm not too late!'

'Let me.' He took the now quiescent bundle from her, produced a penknife from his pocket, and swiftly cut the cords. Then he whipped the sacking away, revealing a small ginger and black kitten with fur clinging wetly to its thin frame. It cowered abjectly on the grass, emitting a thin wail that went straight to Ginny's heart.

'Oh, the poor little thing!'

She stretched out her arms to gather the kitten to her bosom, but Sir Peter stopped this by raising her from the grass and supporting her against the immaculate brown coat he was wearing, much to the detriment of that garment.

'Have a care!' he warned. 'It's terrified, poor creature, and may fly at you. Are you all right? You're wet through, and must be chilled to the bone — here, take this.'

He disengaged himself from her, slipped out of the coat and placed it about her shoulders. Then he looked towards the inn. Seeing an ostler appear in the forecourt, he hailed the man, who came running at once.

'Oh, pay no heed to me!' exclaimed Ginny, with chattering teeth. 'Pray, pray, help the kitten!'

Sir Peter directed the ostler to convey the bedraggled kitten indoors to dry out by the kitchen fire, warning him to use something thick to pick it up for fear of a mauling. He then placed his arm about Ginny and steered her towards the inn.

'We must get you into some dry garments at once, unless you're to take a chill,' he said, briskly, as they reached the door. 'What ho! Landlord!'

The innkeeper came out from the nether regions of his premises, and stared aghast at the sight that met his eyes. There was Sir Peter, usually so well turned-out, standing in his shirt sleeves supporting a young lady wet through, covered in slime and duckweed and from whose clothes a puddle of dirty, evil-smelling water was rapidly forming on his new red carpet which was the pride of the establishment.

'Your wife, man!' said Sir Peter brusquely. 'Miss Turville's fallen in the duckpond, and needs dry garments and a hot drink at once if she isn't to take harm of it — quickly!'

At this, the bemused landlord pulled himself together sufficiently to summon his wife, a sensible, comfortable woman who bore Ginny off with many cluckings and expressions of concern.

'I'll need a wash myself,' said Sir Peter, ruefully surveying his hands and soiled shirt sleeves. 'And afterwards some coffee for us both, I think, Benson, if you'll be so good.'

'Of course, Mr. Peter — that's to say, Sir Peter,' replied Benson, who had known the Martyns all his working life. 'If you'll please to step this way, Sir. Mayhap you'll be wanting to borrow a coat? It won't rightly be what *you* thinks of as a coat, Sir, but I'll vouch for it being clean, and it'll serve till you reach Misbourne House. Will you be needing the coach to take you back, you and the young lady? If so, I'll have the horses set to in readiness.'

Sir Peter agreed that this was a very good plan; and, having had a wash and brush up and donned the borrowed coat with a carefully concealed grimace, sat himself down by the coffee room fire to await the return of Miss Eugenia Turville.

Chapter X

After an interval she appeared, looking much more like her usual self in the best gown belonging to the landlady's second daughter, but with her dark brown hair still clinging in damp curls to her forehead. He rose at her entrance, settling her in a chair close to the fire. The landlady brought some coffee and withdrew, leaving them alone together.

'And now suppose you tell me all about it,' he suggested, when she had sipped some of the hot coffee.

'There's not much to tell. That wretched boy came along with the poor little kitten trussed up in a bundle in his arms, and before I could stop him, he had flung it into the pond. What happened to the boy, by the way?' she asked, suddenly realising that she had forgotten all about him in the pressure of events.

'He took to his heels as if all the devils in hell were after him,' replied Sir Peter laughing. 'And I was too occupied in seeing you safe to think of pursuit.'

She looked at him severely. 'It's no laughing matter, sir. Why should a child — he was little more! — want to do such a cruel thing?'

'Perhaps you must not blame him too much, Miss Turville. He may have been acting under orders. The kitten is a female —' he coughed delicately — 'as I have just been informed by Mrs. Benson. It may not have been considered a welcome addition to the lad's household.'

'If they wanted to be rid of it, they should have given it to some farmer or miller,' pronounced Ginny, emphatically.

'Female cats are excellent mousers, and there's always need for keeping down mice in such places.'

He noticed that her hazel eyes turned almost orange when she became indignant, and found himself fascinated by this.

'True,' he said, smiling. 'But I expect this was the easier way, and they took it, as most of us do, alas.'

'I cannot think why you should defend such actions, sir!'

'Well, it is all supposition, anyway,' he answered gently. 'But life is hard for farm labourers, you know, and perhaps doesn't always encourage gentle emotions towards animals. We can afford the luxury of indulging such feelings, but possibly we shouldn't judge others by our own yardstick.'

She looked at him in silence for a moment, the Ackroyd in her acknowledging his shrewd acceptance of differing attitudes in the social scale. She nodded at last.

'You're right, of course. I've seen enough in Yorkshire to realise that.'

He liked the honesty that compelled her to admit the existence of other points of view than her own. In his experience, most young ladies of Quality had never spent a second's thought on any way of life outside their own experience.

'Yorkshire. Ah, yes.' Their conversation together reminded him of something that had challenged his interest from the start. He looked at her a moment in silence, wondering if he dare broach the subject.

'Yorkshire?' she repeated. 'What do you wish to say on that head, sir?'

'Only this,' he replied, making up his mind. 'Forgive me if I intrude upon ground which you may choose to keep private. But — why do you assume a strong regional accent whenever you're speaking with your relatives? That it must be assumed is clear, for never once have you used it with me today, even in moments of the greatest stress — as, for instance, when I fished you out of the pond.'

'Oh, dear,' she said, weakly, and blushed.

'I beg your pardon — perhaps I shouldn't —'

'No, no.' She waved his diffidence aside. 'You did fish me out of the pond, and for that I owe you something, not even having had the grace to thank you, as yet. It's not an elevating story, I fear, as it shows my relatives and indeed, myself in a far from favourable light. But as you already know *their* part in the affair,' she went on, remembering suddenly that this was true, 'and also suspect mine, perhaps I should confess the whole to you. It will be a relief to do so, because I don't wish you to think me — that is,' she added, in some slight confusion — 'your sister Mrs. Draycott has been so very kind to me, as, indeed, have all your family — oh, dear I'm not telling this very well!'

'Pray take your time,' he recommended her, gently.

'Well, to start at the beginning, which is always the best place — do you recall my cousin here in this inn on Wednesday of last week?'

He nodded, then started a little as the implications of her question began to strike him.

'I see you've guessed,' she said, eyeing him shrewdly. 'Yes, I was also here at that time in this coffee room, sitting with my maid Nancy while we waited for the coach. We heard *every word* that passed between the gentlemen in the adjoining room. I could hardly fail to realise that it was my cousin Frank speaking, and that I was the subject of the conversation; although, of course, I didn't then know who the other two gentlemen were. I realised that later, when I had been introduced to you and Mr. Draycott at the hunt.'

He made no reply, being too occupied with trying to recall his own part in that conversation. He was reasonably certain that he had said nothing that could have given offence to Miss Eugenia. Indeed, his feelings at the time had been all on her side; he, too, had once been a victim of her Aunt's ambitious scheming.

'I dare say I don't need to tell you I was as mad as fire at what I heard!' she went on. 'I have a very quick temper, though it's not really vindictive, and is usually soon spent. I made up my mind then and there to pay them out in their own coin! They made no secret of the fact that they expected me to be a vulgar creature quite beneath their touch, so I determined to live up to their expectations. I meant to make myself so obnoxious to them that my Aunt would be glad to be rid of me as soon as possible! And Aubrey tells me that I've succeeded splendidly — Aunt Sophia would rather have her sons wed to a — a man-eating tiger than to me, now!'

'So you have confided in Aubrey?' he asked.

'Oh, that just came about by accident. You see, he has a secret from his mother, too, so we agreed not to betray each other.'

'You must have become very friendly with that young man.'

There was something in his tone she could not quite fathom. She shrugged.

'I can't pretend to strong feelings of friendship for any of my relatives at Lydeard Hall, sir. In my opinion, their conduct was monstrous! If I *had* been such a milk-and-water innocent as they evidently hoped I was, I should have been shamefully taken in, and coerced into matrimony for no better reason than that I'm an heiress!'

He was silent for a moment, then said, 'I fear that's the way of the world, Miss Turville.'

'Well, it may be, but it's not my way!' she replied, forcefully. 'If I am to wed anyone, I hope it may be someone who will value me for something other than my fortune!'

'You certainly deserve as much,' he said, looking at her with a serious expression.

She felt the colour rising in her cheeks again, and hastily finished her coffee.

'Perhaps we should be getting back,' she said, afterwards. 'By now, the others will be down to breakfast, and they'll wonder where I am.' She sighed. 'Oh, dear, in some ways I wish I'd never embarked on this hoax! It was fun, at first, but now I find it tiresome. I think perhaps I had best make some excuse for going to my godmother in London at once, so that I can be quit of the affair. What do you think, Sir Peter? I know my Aunt would find it as much of a relief as I would.'

'Could you not simply abandon your pose?' he suggested. 'After all, you seem to have made a sufficient protest, by all accounts.'

'But if I do that, it will put my Aunt in charity with me again, and the whole detestable business will start afresh!'

He nodded sympathetically. 'I know — it is vastly disagreeable for you. But as you've already explained matters to Aubrey, why not also take Frank into your confidence? He has a nice sense of humour, and will appreciate the jest, I assure you. And once he realises that you know all about Lady Turville's scheme, you should be quite safe from his attentions — that is —'

He paused, and she looked up questioningly, waiting for him to continue. He seemed reluctant, so she prompted him.

'Yes? You were saying —?'

'That is,' he continued, slowly, avoiding her eyes, 'unless he has begun to value you for yourself alone, just as you would wish.'

'But I wouldn't wish it!' she declared vehemently. 'Oh, I'll allow that of my two cousins I prefer Frank, for he is more amusing, besides having more spirit than Aubrey. But I must tell you that I have no opinion at all of his character!'

He shook his head sadly. 'Poor Frank! Then in that case, he had best not learn to value you. But I know him rather better than you do, if you'll allow me to say so, and I think you're judging him too harshly. Unfortunately, his family seems to bring out the worst in him. Away from their influence, he's no end of a good fellow.'

'Well, I suppose I must take your word for that, though I've yet to see any good qualities in him for myself,' she conceded, reluctantly. 'But perhaps it would be a way out of my difficulty if he were to know all. The only thing is —' she paused, then went on with an uneasy laugh — 'I don't precisely relish the notion of telling him. Oh, I know they deserved to be paid out for their odious attitude towards me, but — but — I greatly fear that I've behaved like a hoyden myself! At any rate, Granpa Ackroyd would say so!'

'Your maternal grandfather, I collect? A man of strict notions?'

She nodded, laughing. 'The strictest! I must be more of a lady for him than for anyone! But possibly,' she continued, looking at Sir Peter with a defiant air, 'you could not understand that anyone engaged in Trade should be so nice in his notions of propriety. No doubt you think as my relatives do —'

'I have always made it a strict rule to endeavour to maintain a habit of *independent* thought,' he said, with a deliberate pomposity belied by the twinkle in his eye. 'To think as others do — that is the ultimate insult, Miss Turville! I am deeply offended.'

'No, you are not.' She laughed again, then impulsively stretched out a hand towards him. 'Oh, you are so *comfortable* to be with, sir! I haven't been so much at ease since I left home.'

He took her hand in a light clasp, hesitated for a moment, then patted it and released it at once.

'I am happy to be of service, ma'am,' he said, with a slight bow. 'Allow me to offer you yet another small service — let me tell Frank for you.'

Her eyes lit up. 'Oh, no, would you truly? That would be so very —' She broke off, the colour coming to her face again. 'But I have no right to trouble you with my concerns, sir. It would be a monstrous imposition —'

'Nonsense, my —' he passed over the dropped word adroitly, changing it to 'ma'am' — 'I've known Frank Turville all my life — nothing could be simpler. He'll think it a splendid jest I promise you, and you'll no longer have any need to act out a part of which you've grown tired. Just leave all to me.'

She was very content to do this; and smiled at him in such a confiding way as he led her out to the carriage he could almost fancy he had a small girl in his charge. There was no doubt that she was an enchanting, unexpected creature, Miss Eugenia Turville.

Chapter XI

Undoubtedly Lady Smallwode's ball was a great success. The carriages that had thronged the street several hours since had disgorged a gratifying number of fashionably attired ladies and gentlemen of high social standing who were now engaged in the pleasant pursuit of dancing to the strains of a well-tuned orchestra. The long pier glasses in the room reflected the myriad colours of the dancers' costumes under the brilliant lights of hundreds of candles set in the cut-glass chandeliers overhead. Even the Prince Regent, his generous figure oozing from the bounds of a tight blue coat and white satin knee breeches, had condescended to put in a brief appearance.

Yet Lady Smallwode frowned as she surveyed the scene, turning a discontented face to her spouse.

'It's too much,' she muttered in his ear. 'Only look at her! What chance has poor Hortensia, I ask you?'

Lord Smallwode knew quite well who was the subject of his wife's complaint, and allowed his eyes to dwell briefly but appreciatively upon a vision in pale blue satin under spangled gauze who was at that moment the centre of a group of admiring gentlemen.

'All the eligible men!' continued his wife, developing her theme. 'She was driving in the Park this afternoon with Myndon, and yesterday it was Bredon! Yes, and the day before —'

'Spare me an account of all the demmed fellows the gal's driven out with, for God's sake!'

'Girl? She's no girl — that's what makes it so bad! She's had her chance, and a prodigious fine chance it was, too, getting an Earl in her grasp! One would think she might have sufficient notion of fair play —'

Lord Smallwode laughed. 'Oh, Gad, m'dear! When have females had any sporting instincts, I ask you? Besides, the young widow can't be blamed if she turns all the men's heads — would have turned mine at their age, I dare say — that is,' he added, hastily, 'if I hadn't met you, of course, m'dear.'

His wife emitted what in a less well-bred woman would have been considered a snort, and turned away to seek consolation in the ruffled bosom of another anxious Mama with a plain daughter to establish creditably.

Meanwhile, Lucilla Ruscombe was enjoying to the full holding court among such a distinguished set of admirers. Why it was that her cool beauty should have the power to inflame men's hearts had often exercised the wits of her many female detractors, but never troubled her mind in the slightest. So it was, and she was content to have it so. Even the burden of a doting husband old enough to be her grandfather had not noticeably decreased her circle of admirers; and she had not been called on to bear the burden for long. The period of mourning had been boring, of course, but discreet companionship had not been quite out of the question. And Lucilla was nothing if not discreet.

Her glance wavered for a moment from Lord Bredon's face to take in the figure of Hortensia Smallwode, her hostess's daughter, standing disconsolately beside her Mama; a moon-faced girl, with plump arms swelling beneath the puff sleeves of her expensive ball gown. Why was it, wondered Lucilla with the incredulity born of perfect taste, that round faced females so often chose elaborate hairstyles featuring masses of curls and bedecked with flowers? And if they must do so, why did not their mothers warn them off, as hers would most certainly have done? But there was no fathoming such mysteries. She brought her gaze back to Lord Bredon's face with such a sweet expression in her china blue eyes that his heart missed a beat, and the other admirers gathered about her found themselves experiencing unwelcome pangs of jealousy. All was well again the next moment, for she had plenty of such looks in her repertoire, and was more than ready to share them around equally.

She passed a pleasant evening dancing with all her admirers and to their despair never favouring one above another. Then she thanked her by now sour-faced hostess with real sincerity, trod the few carpeted steps to the street and mounted into her carriage. Arrived at the late Earl's town house, she went languidly upstairs to where her maid was waiting to undress her.

When she was in a loose muslin peignoir with her corn coloured hair loose about her shoulders, she took up a letter which had been lying unopened all day on her dressing table. She had recognised her mother's handwriting at once that morning and had been in no hurry to open the missive, anticipating no pleasure from perusing its contents. Now she skipped through it, pausing every now and then to look at herself critically in the mirror. Mama had a tiresome girl staying from Yorkshire, the daughter of Uncle Edward, who had married into Trade. The girl was vulgar — well, what could Mama expect? Emmeline had sprained her ankle ... Could that be a spot forming at the side of her nose? She must ask Simmons for the Denmark lotion ... Mama would be so relieved if her dear Lucy could make it convenient to come home for a short time to chaperone this odious girl ... No, it was not a spot, it was a freckle. A *freckle*! That was almost worse! Next they would be calling her a milkmaid! Strawberries, that was the thing; crushed strawberries. Not easy to get at this season, but still, something drastic must be done about freckles ... It might interest Lucy to know — unlikely, thought Lucilla cynically — that Peter Martyn was at Misbourne House for his sister Eleanor's wedding —

Now her interest was really caught. Peter Martyn ... She forgot about the freckle, and read the letter through again, carefully this time. When she had finished, she allowed it to drop from her fingers and sat staring into the mirror, for once not seeing the lovely image before her. Peter Martyn ...

Returned from the wars, and still unmarried. Her thoughts drifted back four years. She saw again his sensitive face and the grey eyes warmed by that special smile which she could always bring to his lips. She felt once more that stirring of the pulses that his presence alone had ever had the power to rouse in her. She felt it, and she marvelled. Four years, and a mere memory could do so much?

She placed slim white fingers against her face, and saw in the mirror that they shook slightly. Of course, if one had not had ambition... And if it had not been for Mama's influence, what would ambition have mattered beside that inexplicable magnetism, that yearning of heart for heart?

She sat there a long time before she finally prepared for bed. But her mind was quite made up; tomorrow, she would cancel all her engagements and go down to Buckinghamshire.

A ray of pale sunlight filtered through the stained glass window, reflecting a touch of blue on the bride's ivory satin gown, as she came down the aisle on the arm of her tall, distinguished looking brother.

If only her father could have lived to take Peter's place beside our little Nellie, thought Lady Martyn, feeling the tears stinging her eyes and fighting hard to keep them back. Oh, don't let me cry, please God, don't let me cry! And bless them always, this young couple, through all the joys and sorrows, laughter and tears that make up a marriage; until they, too, are handing their children into the care of someone else, someone outside the family on whom all their future hopes of happiness will depend. I can do nothing now, she thought. I have loved and tended, watched and guarded, but now I can only pray that her husband will give her all the loving care for which she once depended on us. May she be more fortunate than her brother, my poor Peter — and God bless Peter, too, and bring him happiness at last.

These thoughts and emotions found their echo across the aisle of the church in the bosom of the bridegroom's mother, who clutched her handkerchief nervously and hoped she would not have recourse to it. The bridegroom's father, a West country squire of ancient lineage, patted her arm reassuringly and regarded the young couple at the altar with a softer look than was usual with him. Deuced fine girl, Eleanor Martyn, and never been in prettier looks than today. A good match for young Greg in every way. Pity the War was over — not much for a young Naval Captain to do at present. Marriage would keep him occupied for a time, of course, then perhaps he would take an interest in the estate. Only son — time he did; outdoor type, too, not like some of these Bond St. Beaux. Only look at that precious pair of Turville's. The elder wasn't so bad, bruising rider to hounds, good sportsman; but that younger cub, Aubrey or some such devilish name — faugh! he was enough to turn a man's stomach! At this point, recollecting where he was, he cleared his throat and for a moment wore the look of a schoolboy caught talking during the service in chapel.

It must be admitted that the despised Aubrey's mind was not fixed on the ceremony at all. The church at Great Lydeard was full on this special day, but Mr. and Mrs. Mandeville and their daughter Henrietta were not among the congregation, as their acquaintance with the Martyns was very slight. Aubrey was nursing a hope that when the ceremony and the succeeding wedding breakfast should be over, there would still be time enough for him to keep a tryst with Hetty in a secluded spot not far from her home in Wendover. That was, if he could escape from his family without too many questions.

He glanced at his mother, who appeared neither moved nor particularly interested in the ceremony taking place; and then at his father, looking very correct, but with his mind — if Aubrey was any judge — firmly fixed on the enjoyment of a glass or two of wine afterwards. Frank seemed to be watching their cousin Eugenia more often than he was attending to the service. Perhaps while they were all caught up with friends and neighbours after the wedding breakfast, reflected Aubrey, it might be possible for him to slip away unheeded.

Eugenia was conscious of Frank's sidelong looks at her, and she stirred irritably. How could anyone, even someone as cynical as her cousin fail to be moved by the beautiful words of this ancient ceremony? 'From this day forward, for better for worse ... to love and to cherish, till death us do part...'

She would willingly say that for the right man, some day, she thought. She looked, not for the first time, at Peter Martyn, and once again that disturbing emotion surged up in her. So she *was* falling in love with him, she admitted to herself, dismayed. What could she do about it? Was there any hope for her?

If she could have seen into Sir Peter's mind at that moment, she would have acknowledged defeat. For he was thinking of the past and of Lucilla.

Chapter XII

Matters did not fall out well for Aubrey. A young lady was present whom Lady Turville, quite decided by now that Eugenia would not be suited to either of her sons, considered would be an eminently desirable match for Aubrey. She contrived to have him seated by this damsel, a tall, thin girl with lack-lustre hair and a depressed look, during the meal which followed the ceremony. When he made one or two furtive attempts to slip away as the festivities drew to a close, he found his mother's compelling eye upon him on each occasion. He was forced to remain, trying to maintain a boring conversation which could not give any pleasure either to himself or to the young lady. When the Turville's carriage arrived he was unable to make good his escape and was ordered inside to sit with his mother and Eugenia, while Frank and his father returned home in Frank's curricle.

Later on, during that evening, he contrived a quiet word with Eugenia to enlist her support.

'If you will but say that you'd like me to drive you out tomorrow, my mother will raise no objection, nor plague me with questions,' he pleaded.

'That's all very well, Aubrey, but how long do you mean to go on in this way?' she objected. 'I shan't be staying here above another fortnight, and what excuse will you find to offer then?'

'I shall return to Town, where I can be my own master,' he answered, sulkily, 'And go to see her when I choose.'

'You can be so now, any time you decide to take a firm stand. Only consider, Aubrey — you are three and twenty, not a youth in your teens.'

'Oh, for God's sake; have done!' he exclaimed, with a flash of anger. 'Females are all the same — they must nag a fellow. Well, most of them, anyway,' he amended, thinking of his Henrietta, who would have considered it little short of heresy to question anything he chose to do.

She suppressed a smile, knowing very well what his thoughts were, and agreed to drive out with him on the following day.

''Pon my word, Cousin Eugenia, I'm in a fair way to calling out my own brother,' said Frank, coming to sit beside her as Aubrey moved away. 'Did I just hear you promising him the pleasure of your company tomorrow? This is to show too much partiality, you know — with anyone but Aubrey, you would be hopelessly compromised.'

'Eh, you talk like a great gowk!' she retorted, laughing.

'And you talk like a mill lass — but only when it suits you, I fancy,' he replied in a low tone, with a twinkle in his eye.

She looked guilty. 'So you do know — did — did — Sir Peter —'

He nodded. 'Yes, Peter Martyn revealed your secret to me yesterday at the wedding reception. But I think, my dear Ginny — I understand you prefer to be called Ginny? — I think I'd begun to guess for myself. You were so obviously enjoying yourself, as though at some private joke. And then there were times, y'know, when you lapsed into disappointingly conventional style — oh, yes, you soon corrected yourself, but it was sufficient to make me wonder if you were up to something. I must confess I couldn't quite see what; but you may have noticed that once or twice I gave you some positive encouragement to continue with those endless monologues of yours.'

'Yes, to be sure I did, and I knew why, too,' she rejoined, spiritedly. 'It was because you encourage anything that promotes mischief among your family!'

He gave her a whimsical look. 'Ah, so you've divined my character,' he said, sadly. 'And so early in our acquaintance, too. It must be my earnest endeavour to give you a better notion of me. But — dare I say it? — surely this is a case of the pot calling the kettle black? Haven't you yourself been promoting a little mischief?'

'And why?' demanded Ginny, fiercely. 'Just ask yourself that, sir! I suppose Sir Peter must have told you that I overheard every word of your conversation that day in the Lydeard Arms?'

Frank nodded, looking at her with unaccustomed seriousness. 'Yes. And I admit freely that I've rarely felt so shamefaced over anything. Can you possibly believe, Ginny, that those remarks were made in a spirit of levity, and not with malice?'

'No.' Her reply was instant and uncompromising. 'No female who has been called a *Yorkshire Pudding* is likely to overlook the fact readily.'

'But my dear girl —' his brows arched in a look of comical dismay — 'I saw how ridiculous such a description was the moment I set eyes on you! Damme, I was only out to raise a laugh with my companions!'

'At my expense,' she reminded him, drily.

'Oh, yes, but I didn't know you, then! When I saw how lovely, how charming —'

'Flattery won't prosper your cause,' said Ginny, severely, but now there was a twinkle in her eye.

He saw it, and relaxed. 'Then there is nothing left for me but to put a period to my existence,' he said, sadly.

'Well, if you do that, Cousin, don't choose to drown yourself in the pond at Great Lydeard.' She held her nose with a grimace. 'I cannot at all recommend it after my own experience of those waters!'

'I heard about that, too, from Peter Martyn. He thought you a most intrepid character.'

'Most likely he thought me a hoyden! But when I'm indignant about anything, I cannot sit idly by and do nothing. I know that it's far more elegant to do so, but I've never rated elegance above humanity.'

He smiled at her, thinking not for the first time how refreshing she was after the insipid females who were annually launched by their Mamas on the London social scene. He himself was not a conventional man; and it had been the prospect of settling down for life with one of these tiresomely proper young ladies which had so far turned his thoughts resolutely away from matrimony. But his cousin Eugenia, now...

Lady Turville observed that Francis was dutifully keeping her exhausting guest engaged in quiet conversation, and felt duly grateful to him. Anything was preferable to enduring one of Eugenia's monologues after all the boredom of Eleanor Martyn's wedding. She reflected that she really must be feeling her age at last, since lately so many trivial matters had played on the raw edges of her nerves. Perhaps she had been foolish to tax herself with the business of trying to promote an advantageous marriage for one of her sons. Surely it was enough that she had married off her two daughters creditably?

But the affair had seemed so simple when she had first thought of it, so well within her grasp. She sighed; she had done, she would concern herself no further. Of course, if Lucilla and Peter Martyn *did* make a match of it, there could be no possible objection nowadays. And as for Aubrey, perhaps that lanky Annabel Truscott would do; after all, she had a fortune of twenty thousand pounds. Not quite so impressive as Eugenia's expectations, to be sure, but respectable enough for Aubrey. She looked again at Frank and Eugenia with a speculative eye. Was it possible that —? But no, she had done with matchmaking for good. They must all shift for themselves. And as for Eugenia, the sooner she went to her godmother in London, the better.

On the following morning it looked as if the recent unseasonably fine weather had come to an end, for the sky was overcast.

'You surely don't intend to go out in Aubrey's curricle today?' Emmeline asked incredulously, when she heard this project mentioned at breakfast. 'Only look at the weather, Eugenia — you'll be in for a wetting, for sure. Mama, don't you agree?'

Lady Turville looked up from the delicately perfumed letter she was reading. 'What's that you say, Emmeline? My dear, the most splendid news! This is from Lucilla, and she will be with us today! Could anything be more fortunate?'

'Well, I am sure it's not be wondered at, since you wrote asking her to come,' retorted Emmeline, acidly. 'If she's to be here, I may as well return home. I'll send a message to Welwyn, and he can come over to fetch me in the carriage. My ankle is much improved, and there are a dozen matters awaiting my attention there.'

Her mother uttered a civil protest, but without much force. Emmeline was the least favourite of her offspring. In the discussion that followed, Ginny and Aubrey were able to slip away without any further notice being taken of them.

'Your sister's right, you know,' said Ginny, regarding the sky, as she settled herself in the curricle beside her cousin. 'We shall most likely have rain before long.'

'Never fear, Ginny, we can always find shelter,' replied Aubrey, optimistically. 'I don't think it will come to anything but a shower, myself. We often get these dull days at this time of year.'

She was far from being a delicate plant that feared rough weather, so cheerfully accepted his optimistic assurance, which was justified during the duration of their drive to Wendover. As they turned into the yard of the Red Lion, however, a light drizzle began to fall. At once, Aubrey was all consternation for his lady love.

'This is the deuce of a coil! What's to be done? Not for anything would I have Hetty exposed to a wetting, and already she'll be on her way to our rendezvous — it's too late to stop her.'

'Then you'd best leave me here, and take the curricle to meet her. With the hood up, it won't be too bad, it's only a drizzle, not a downpour.'

He shook his head. 'The hood will offer precious little protection if it comes on hard, as it may do at any minute. Besides, I can't very well leave you here unattended. M'mother would raise no end of a dust if I did anything so shabby.'

'Oh, as to that,' shrugged Ginny, 'I don't regard it in the least. I dare say there may be a private parlour where I can sit. Yes, that would be the thing, and then you can bring Miss Mandeville back here, and it will all be perfectly proper, because I shall act as chaperone for her. Only you'd best make haste, Aubrey.'

He demurred again. 'I suppose there's nothing else to be done, but I don't care overmuch for bringing her here, because she and her family are so well known in the town.'

'Well, either that,' said Ginny, impatiently, 'or else you take her straight back home, while I await you here. Come, here is the ostler looking for your orders.'

This persuaded her cousin to make up his mind. While the ostler looked after the curricle, Aubrey entered the inn and Eugenia was soon installed in a small private parlour at the back of the house. It was all the work of a few minutes; and then Aubrey returned to his vehicle and swept under the archway into the street as though pursued by hobgoblins, as Ginny reflected with a smile.

It was not very long before he returned with Miss Mandeville, looking very pretty in a warm russet riding dress and a hat to match. She greeted Ginny shyly then seemed at a loss for something to say. Aubrey left them alone for a few moments while he conferred with the landlord.

'I trust you didn't get too wet?' asked Ginny.

'Oh — oh, thank you, no,' replied Hetty, rather breathlessly. 'It does not rain very hard, and Mr. Turville brought me in his curricle.'

'Perhaps it will stop soon,' continued Ginny, glancing from the window at the unrelenting grey sky. 'What a pity it should have spoilt your ride.'

She intended no sarcasm, but Hetty Mandeville blushed painfully and returned no answer.

'Unless it does stop soon,' went on Ginny, trying to retrieve the position, 'you'll be unable to return home on horseback. We must think what is to be done.'

'Oh, but Mr. Turville is at this moment arranging for all that,' stammered Hetty. 'I think he intends to hire a carriage from the landlord, and leave the curricle here for the present.'

Ginny raised her eyebrows. 'He does? I had no notion that he could be so resourceful.'

'Forgive me, Miss Turville, but that must be because you do not know him very well,' replied Hetty, with more assurance. 'I am sure I always feel complete confidence in Mr. Turville's ability to deal with every situation.'

'You do?'

Hetty nodded emphatically. 'I am rather stupid, you know, and inclined to be nervous at — oh, so many little things! I dare say you'd laugh at me, if you knew. My brothers do — Papa, too, sometimes. But your cousin is so — so wise, and yet always so understanding. I know of no other gentleman who has lived so much in fashionable society and yet can have patience with my foolishness.'

These remarks tended to turn Ginny's stomach and at the same time threatened to overcome her gravity. Aubrey wise and understanding! Well, she had yet to see it! Her curiosity aroused, she proceeded to draw the girl out further on the subject. She soon saw that in Miss Mandeville's eyes Aubrey was a veritable man of the world deserving the utmost respect and admiration. At first amused, Ginny gradually began to realise that Aubrey might have done much worse for himself than allow his fancy to light on this shrinking little creature; perhaps she brought out in him talents and virtues which would always remain hidden under the influence of a more strong-minded female, on the pattern of his own mother and elder sister.

The subject of their conversation soon returned to announce that he had been successful in obtaining a carriage. Hetty's groom was to return to her home with the horses, explaining that her friends Mr. Aubrey and Miss Eugenia Turville would be bringing her safely back in a very short time.

Thereafter, although refreshments were brought in, the party lacked spirit. It was evident that the two young people had much they wished to say to one another, but found conversation difficult in Eugenia's presence. For her part, she heartily wished herself away, without well knowing where she could go in the circumstances. Her presence was needed for propriety's sake, particularly as Miss Mandeville and her family were well known at the Red Lion. Aubrey, too, seemed to feel the futility of prolonging the interlude, and soon announced his intention of conveying Hetty home. Accordingly, they left the parlour to make their way to the courtyard where their hired carriage was waiting.

As they reached the entrance hall, they encountered a middle-aged lady and gentleman, both in riding dress, who had that moment entered the inn. They greeted Hetty Mandeville with the familiarity of long standing acquaintances, and she was obliged to stop and introduce Aubrey and Eugenia to them.

'Have you been interrupted in your ride by the weather?' asked the gentleman, whose name was Vyner. 'So have we — we took no heed of it at first, but now it's coming down in earnest, so we thought it best to take shelter until it's passed over.'

Ginny looked beyond them through the door, and saw that the drizzle had turned to a steady downpour.

'You were more fortunate in the weather last Saturday, Henrietta,' put in Mrs. Vyner, with a meaning smile. 'You were able to take a stroll up the lane leading to Bacombe Hall. I was out with the dog, and recognised you from the distance, though I don't believe you saw me.'

It was in character for Henrietta to blush, but Ginny could not help feeling annoyed with her for it. Aubrey managed to put an end politely but firmly to the conversation, and escorted both the young ladies to the waiting coach under the shelter of an umbrella borrowed from the landlord.

'Oh, dear!' exclaimed Hetty, with a look of dismay, once they were seated inside. 'What is to be done? Mrs. Vyner will tell Mama the very next time they meet, and that must be before long, since they are neighbours of ours.'

In her consternation, she did not bother to attempt any concealment of the situation in front of Eugenia; and in spite of Aubrey's patting her hand and telling her not to trouble her little head about anything she was obviously still uneasy when they parted from her a few minutes later at her own door. She politely invited them to go in with her, but Aubrey thought it more prudent to refuse.

'Well, I hope you're satisfied,' remarked Ginny as they drove home. 'You have placed that poor little creature in an intolerable situation!'

He coloured. 'Oh, it's all a hum! I dare say that Vyner female will never mention the business, after all; and if she does, Hetty has only to say that it was an accidental meeting, and there's an end to it. The pity is that she's so gentle, she is easily alarmed.'

'All the more reason for you to protect her,' stated Ginny vigorously. 'Do you realise that she thinks of you as something of a cross between St. George and Sir Galahad?'

'She does?' asked Aubrey, pleased.

'Heaven alone knows why, for to my mind you bear more resemblance to Sir Andrew Aguecheek!'

But fortunately Aubrey was not so well read as his cousin, and had never heard of the comic character from Shakespeare's play Twelfth Night; so although Ginny had certainly given him food for thought, she had not mortally wounded his vanity.

Chapter XIII

It was later on that same day when the weather had cleared that a light travelling carriage with a crest on its panels drew up before Lydeard Hall. Judging from the quantity of baggage which it carried, one might have expected a large family to step down from the luxuriously padded blue leather interior. Instead, one slim, elegant young lady descended, fashionably attired in a green velvet pelisse trimmed with ermine and a high crowned bonnet ruched with matching green ribbon. From beneath the wide brim of the bonnet pale gold hair framed a face of almost startling beauty, with classical features and china blue eyes. The male servants handed her down with alacrity and such exaggerated care that she might have been some precious and fragile work of art; and her abigail, a plain, elderly woman with a sharp face, also hovered anxiously about her.

'If you would just take my muff, Carter,' murmured the lady, removing one hand from a large white ermine muff, but otherwise making no move to pass it over to her attendant.

The maid drew nearer at once, and gently disengaged the muff from her mistress's loose grasp. Lady Ruscombe paid no more heed than if an insect had passed by, and, resting her gloved hand lightly on the footman's arm, ascended the steps to her parents' door.

'My dear Lucilla!' exclaimed Lady Turville in fulsome accents as she rose from a chair to plant a peck on her younger daughter's cheek. 'How delightful to see you here! You had a good journey, I trust?'

'Tedious,' replied Lady Ruscombe, in a languorous drawl. 'How are you, Mama? And you, Emmeline?' she added, allowing her sister's lips to approach within almost half an inch of that classic, flawless countenance.

She directed a mildly inquiring glance at Eugenia, who had out of courtesy risen to her feet on her cousin's entrance. Lady Turville performed the necessary introductions, and the two young ladies greeted each other with proper civility, but a marked lack of enthusiasm. An astute glance from Lucilla's deceptively limpid blue eyes informed her that her cousin Eugenia would offer no rivalry to herself, being in a totally different style, more an artless child of nature, so to speak. On her side, Ginny realised with sinking spirits why it was that Sir Peter Martyn had been besotted with this female. Surely few men could resist such a flawless beauty?

The civilities being over, Lucilla removed to her bedchamber to repair the ravages of her short journey from Town. She did not appear again until close on the dinner hour suitably not to say enchantingly attired in a blue satin gown which echoed the colour of her eyes. Her father embraced her with genuine affection, but the greetings between herself and her two brothers were restrained to the point of coolness. During dinner Lady Turville questioned Lucilla on the latest London fashions and gave her a short account of the Misbourne House wedding.

'What was Eleanor wearing?' asked Lucilla, in a tone which showed little real interest in the answer.

'Oh, ivory satin, made high to the neck with insets of Honiton lace,' replied Lady Turville in much the same tone. 'She looked quite well, Peter Martyn gave her away, of course. He is not much changed from when you saw him last, I think.'

'Nonsense, my dear,' interposed her husband. 'Four years fighting in the Peninsula are bound to change any man. He's gained in maturity, wouldn't you say, Frank?'

'Doubtless you're right, sir, but I wonder if that was quite what my mother meant.'

Ginny wondered, too, for she had seen the significant glance that accompanied Lady Turville's words. Obviously some message was being conveyed to Lucilla by that glance. A message of acquiescence in any intentions her daughter might have towards resuming the old relationship with Sir Peter? It was not unlikely.

The following morning brought an opportunity for Ginny to speculate further on this subject. The Draycotts, accompanied by Sir Peter, rode over to Lydeard Hall to take their leave, as they were to return to their own home later in the day. She soon felt that the compliment was all for herself, as Meg spoke very little to anyone else and was very pressing in her cordial invitation to Eugenia to pay them a visit when she would be staying later on with her godmother in Town.

Sir Peter was chiefly occupied in chatting to the other men who were present, but once he turned to Ginny with a reminiscent smile.

'Remember the kitten you rescued the other day? You'll be happy to know that Benson's wife has offered it permanent residence in the stables at the inn. I chanced to be that way yesterday, and thought I'd drop in to enquire after your protégée.'

Ginny's eyes lit up. 'Oh, splendid! It was good of you to take the trouble.'

'Not at all. I felt I must know the fate of an animal for which you had risked life and limb.'

'Hardly that! The greatest risk I took was that of contracting some putrid fever —' she wrinkled her nose expressively — 'from immersion in your local waters.'

'They are certainly not to be compared with those of Harrogate or Bath,' he replied with an air of judicial gravity. 'But I trust they have not given you a total disgust of this area.'

'Far from it — I think Buckinghamshire is delightful — softer and mellower than my native countryside, more of a quiet, domestic beauty. Each has its own particular charm.'

Francis, who had been idly listening to their interchange, now joined in. 'Enhanced, my dear cousin, by your presence,' he said, with a bow.

Sir Peter considered him gravely for a moment, then smiled.

'Oh, no doubt you mean to be odiously cynical again!' exclaimed Ginny, laughing.

'On the contrary,' replied Frank, giving her a meaning glance, 'I was completely sincere.'

She coloured a little, partly with annoyance; but at that moment a diversion occurred. The door opened to admit Lucilla, cool and remote in a white muslin morning gown. She entered with the poise of perfect self-assurance, and spoke a low 'Good morning.'

The visiting gentlemen came at once to their feet, their gaze fixed upon her. Frank's mouth twitched cynically, but Eugenia did not notice. She was watching Sir Peter.

After a momentary flicker of light in his eyes, soon gone, his countenance revealed little. He bowed, smiled and spoke a conventional word of greeting; but Lucilla extended a slim, white hand and looked up at him with all the magnetism of those clear blue eyes.

'Peter!' Her usual drawl was invested with a little more energy. 'How nice to see you — it's been so long.'

'Yes, indeed.'

His tone was noncommittal. He drew back a little to allow Meg and her husband to exchange greetings with the new arrival, and soon everyone was seated again. The conversation was smooth but trivial; after five minutes or so, the visitors rose to depart.

'You will be so quiet, Sir Peter, when all your guests have left you,' remarked Lady Turville. 'You must look in on us whenever you wish.'

He bowed and said she was most kind.

'Well, we are old friends and neighbours, you know,' persisted Lady Turville. 'Bring your Mama and come and dine with us one evening soon — do you chance to be at liberty tomorrow, for instance?'

With some civil show of regret, Sir Peter declined tomorrow.

'Well, perhaps Monday, then? Monday is not generally a day when one has many social engagements. We shall have Emmeline's husband with us, so we would be a comfortable party. Welwyn comes to take Emmeline back home, alas. We shall miss her, but we quite realise that she can ill be spared from home.'

Again Frank looked cynical, but Ginny's eyes were still on Sir Peter. Without being churlish, it would have been difficult for him to refuse this second invitation. He said, therefore, that subject to consulting his mother, he would be happy to dine with them on Monday. An hour was fixed, goodbyes were spoken, and the party from Misbourne House left.

As soon as they had gone, Lady Turville turned to Lucilla.

'Did you find him much changed?'

Her daughter shrugged. 'A little perhaps.'

She gave no encouragement to her mother to continue with that topic, and Lady Turville wisely took the hint.

'I dare say Lucilla, you will like to renew your acquaintance with some other of our neighbours, too,' she continued. 'We must make some calls tomorrow — your cousin Eugenia has met very few people so far, except for the Martyns and the hunting set.'

'Calls — oh, yes,' replied Lucilla, languidly, stifling a yawn. 'But there is no one whom I am particularly anxious to see, Mama. One grows away, you know, after four years. All my friends are in Town nowadays.'

'Do tell me, Lucy,' said Francis, in a mocking tone, 'are *any* of them females?'

She gave him a cool smile. 'My dear brother, are you still intent on shooting your little poison darts at people? You will find the exercise sadly wasted on me, I promise you. I rarely allow myself to become ruffled — it is so fatiguing.'

During the rest of the day, Ginny did her best to try and improve her acquaintance with her lovely cousin; but her efforts at conversation met with little success. Lucilla was ready enough with small talk and did show some signs of animation when fashion was the topic, but anything of a more personal nature failed to rouse a response. Ginny had frequently found that an individual's taste in reading would offer some clue to character, but she found no satisfaction on this occasion. Lucilla said that she never seemed to find the time for reading.

'Oh, yes, I belong to the circulating library and am regularly supplied with the latest novels, of course. They must be seen on one's tables. But for the most part they go back unopened, for there's always something to do in London, you know.'

'But only think what you must miss! Do you mean to say that you have never read that delightful novel *Pride and Prejudice*, which came out a few years back while I was still at school? I am eagerly awaiting a new one called *Emma* by the same author. It appeared recently, but I haven't yet had my copy. I can hardly wait to lay hands on it!'

'Oh, well, one has heard of these novels naturally,' was the languid reply. 'But I fear I am not at all bookish. In fact, I have a horror of bookish females, do not you?'

This seemed too direct a snub to be ignored, so Ginny left the two sisters more or less to their own devices for the rest of that day. She strolled for a while in the gardens before dinner, choosing a gravel path that was not too wet from the rain earlier in the day. To her surprise, she was soon joined by Francis.

'Do you mind if I take a turn with you?' he asked. 'I imagine we both feel the need of a little fresh air.'

She gave her permission though truth to tell she wanted to be alone in order to sort out her thoughts.

'Well,' asked Frank with his usual cynical expression, 'and pray what do you think of my sister Ruscombe?'

'She is very beautiful,' replied Ginny promptly.

'That, yes, oh, certainly. But do you like her?'

'How can I possibly say? I've but this moment met her. She seems very amiable.'

'My dear cousin, you must surely have seen by now that we are none of us truly amiable.'

'The more shame to you to speak so of your own flesh and blood!' retorted Ginny.

'Yes, ain't it? But you see, dear Coz, I've never been one for humbug; and your coming into our family circle has shown me how greatly my own family relies upon that precious commodity. We are all hollow people behind the fashionable façade, Ginny. Beware of us, fly our contact, lest you, too, should become tainted with the Curse of the Turvilles.'

He struck an attitude as he said the last words.

'Shades of Mrs. Radcliffe!' exclaimed Ginny, in the same lighthearted vein. 'I don't know about humbug, Cousin, but you certainly excel at nonsense.'

'Like most nonsense, I think you'll find it contains more than a grain of truth, however. Already, you see, you have lost that charming Yorkshire accent which you had when you first came among us.'

'Eh, lad, but it's nobbut round t'corner, think on!'

He laughed, taking her hand into the crook of his arm. She was quite content to leave it there for the moment; of all her cousins, she certainly liked Francis best, she told herself.

Chapter XIV

Ginny was a good deal in Lucilla's company on the following day, however. Lady Turville ordered out the carriage to embark on the promised series of short morning calls in the neighbourhood, and the four ladies set off together, leaving the menfolk to their own devices. A significant look from Aubrey gave Ginny a clue as to what he meant to do with his time, and she could only feel relieved that for once she was not called on to provide an excuse for his clandestine excursions. Hers was an essentially straightforward disposition that disliked subterfuge.

For the most part, Ginny found the Turvilles' neighbours agreeable people. She had already met some of them at Eleanor Martyn's wedding, and now had an opportunity to improve that brief acquaintance. Several of the young ladies of about her own age were obviously more than a little interested in the appearance in the neighbourhood of such an eligible bachelor as Sir Peter Martyn. One, a saucy looking girl of nineteen or twenty, actually had the temerity to question Lucilla about her past friendship with the gentleman.

'Oh, yes,' replied Lucilla, coolly, looking through her interrogator in a way which Ginny thought worthy of being included in any instructions for depressing impertinent pretensions. 'I did know Sir Peter quite well at one time. We and the Martyns were all playfellows as children.'

The girl caught her mother's eye, blushed, and was silent.

'It's plain to see,' remarked Lady Turville on their return journey, 'that we are too well known here for any of our concerns to escape comment. It has its drawbacks.'

'It is what I so particularly dislike about the country,' agreed Lucilla, with more animation than usual.

'And, pray, are matters so much better in Town?' demanded Emmeline, leaping to the defence of her own way of life. 'All those malicious *on dits* — you know very well London is a hotbed of gossip!'

'But it at least has the merit of being *entertaining* gossip,' drawled Lucilla.

'If you are entertained by hearing another person's reputation torn to shreds, then I have nothing further to say!' snapped Emmeline.

'Can I rely on that, my dear?' replied her sister, in dulcet tones.

'No, really, Lucilla, you are a great deal too bad to tease your sister so!' protested Lady Turville. 'You sound just like Francis in one of his disagreeable moods, and I've had quite enough of that just lately. I declare my nerves are thoroughly overset! Pray let us have no more quarrelling.'

This reproof had the effect of reducing the party to silence, so that it was a relief to Ginny when they arrived back at Lydeard Hall. She was about to go upstairs with the others to remove her outdoor things when she caught sight of Aubrey gesticulating frantically to her from the partly ajar door of the library.

'What is it?' she demanded, entering and closing the door behind her. 'Is something amiss? You look flustered enough.'

'Everything's wrong!' His voice took on the slight whine she had noticed once or twice before when matters were not going well with him. 'It's Hetty — they're going to send her away!'

'Send her away? What do you mean?'

'Her parents — they've discovered that we've been meeting — that confounded female we met at the Red Lion has let the cat out of the bag, and now there's the devil to pay!'

'How have you learnt all this? Have you seen Hetty?'

He shook his head. 'No, there's no chance of that. I turned up as usual this morning at our rendezvous, but she wasn't there. I thought little of it because quite often there are times when one or other of us can't manage to get away. After hanging about a bit, I had just decided to go when I saw her groom galloping hell for leather towards me. He thrust a note from Hetty into my hand, said he daren't stop, and was away again before I could recollect myself sufficiently to ask him what it was all about. I must say, it took me some time to find out from the letter, for poor little Hetty had evidently been in great distress when she wrote it.'

'I imagine she might,' said Ginny, severely. 'She must have had a severe scolding for behaving so improperly; and it's all to be laid at your door, in fact! Where are they sending her?'

'To a devilish strait-laced old aunt in Bristol,' replied Aubrey, glumly. 'Bristol — I ask you! What chance is there now for us to see each other, when a distance of that kind is involved? And even if I do go down there, Hetty says she will be kept so close even her own brother will have difficulty in securing an audience. What's to be done, Eugenia — Ginny, I mean? You're my only friend in this business, y'know, so for Heavens' sake think of something.'

Ginny gave him a scornful look. 'There's only one thing to be done, and you know very well what it is,' she said, with emphasis.

His look of dismay was almost comical. 'You mean declare myself to her parents? But what's the use in that? My own would never consider the match — we talked of this before, if you remember.'

'Aubrey, how serious *are* you about Miss Mandeville?'

'Oh, God, Ginny, there's no other girl in the world for me, assure you! She's so gentle, so sweet — she's not always nagging a fellow, or trying to make him feel a fool by flirting with other men. I've seen scores of young females in London, but never one to touch her for amiability. And she's lovely, too — you must agree about that.'

Ginny nodded. 'Indeed she is. And I must say, Aubrey, that I think she's very well suited to you.'

Aubrey coloured a little with pleasure.

'You do?'

'Yes. It would not do at all for you to marry a strong-minded, Amazon type of creature.'

He shuddered. 'Good God, No! It doesn't bear thinking of!'

'Well, as we're agreed on that,' went on Ginny, in somewhat dogmatic tones, 'surely you think it's worth making some effort to gain such a prize?'

'Confound it, of course I do! Only if by "some effort" you mean tackling my parents on the subject. I can only tell you again that such a course would be hopeless! No one should know better than you that Mother intends both Frank and myself to marry heiresses. That was why she was thrusting me at that devilish Truscott female at Eleanor Martyn's wedding. As though anyone who had seen Hetty could possibly find the Truscott wench worth a second glance!'

'What matters here is not your Mother's intentions, but your *own*. If you make those clear to Hetty's father, I consider the business will be as good as settled. Once you're officially engaged to her, I feel quite sure that for very shame your parents would not cut you off financially. Why don't you confide in your sister Emmeline? She's very fond of you, and would, I'm sure, lend you powerful support with your parents.'

He considered for a moment. 'It's true that Em's a good friend to me,' he said, at last, 'but she has very little influence with Mother. Lucilla has more — but she wouldn't stir herself to help anyone.'

'Then you must manage on your own,' said Ginny, vigorously.

He looked dubious. 'I don't know, though. Perhaps it would be a good idea to tell Em all about it. By what she was saying to me only yesterday, Mother is not now so set on either Frank or myself making a match of it with you. Indeed, Em said she seemed quite dispirited, declaring that she had finished with any attempts to help us to a creditable marriage.'

Ginny laughed with great enjoyment. 'Oh, how famous! Then I've succeeded in what I set out to do — which was to give my Aunt a thorough disgust of me! And it may not have served you a bad turn, either, if only you will be resolute and make a push to take advantage of it. Faint heart, you know, and all that!'

He grinned at her and moved by a sudden rush of gratitude, seized her hand to press it between both his own.

At that precise moment, his mother entered the room.

There can be no doubt that Aubrey's simple gesture, innocent though it was, could have been misleading to anyone who had not heard the previous conversation Lady Turville thought she understood well enough; but instead of the triumph that should have accompanied this sign of the success of her matchmaking scheme, she found herself experiencing dismay. This impossible, vulgar girl! Even the huge fortune which would come with her could scarcely compensate poor Aubrey for the social ostracism which must surely follow their marriage! She was so put out that she snapped at the pair in a way which was usually reserved for her more intimate moments alone with her offspring.

'The idea! Aubrey — Eugenia — it will not at all do to be creeping off together in this style! It is one thing to drive about the countryside in an open carriage, and quite another to shut yourselves up in a room with no one else present! I excuse you, Niece —' there was nothing exculpatory about her tone, however — 'I excuse *you* on the grounds of ignorance of what constitutes proper behaviour for a female of your years. But you, Aubrey, can have no such excuse — you know very well how a gentleman should behave, and while you are under your parents' roof, I will thank you to observe the usages of Polite Society!'

She paused for breath while her two victims exchanged wary glances.

'You may leave us, Aubrey,' she continued, with a regal air. 'And as for you, Eugenia, I am sure you will wish to remove your bonnet and tidy yourself for luncheon.'

Aubrey went out at the first words; but although his air was hangdog enough, he did not feel too depressed. Evidently there was something in what his sister Emmeline had told him yesterday; it really looked as if his mother no longer desired him to make up to Ginny. That being so, there might be a faint hope of reconciling her to a match between himself and Hetty Mandeville. A very faint hope, he thought, with a sudden unwelcome loss of confidence. What had Ginny said? 'Faint heart never won fair lady.' That put him in mind, too, of something else she had said recently; something about Hetty thinking he was another St. George, or some such nonsense!

Dash it all, he could not let the little creature down! He would have a try at it, come what may.

Chapter XV

Aubrey was not seen again until he joined the rest of the family later around the dinner table. Eugenia cast a shrewd eye over him and concluded that he was feeling reasonably pleased with himself at present. She wondered if he had visited the Mandevilles during the afternoon, but had no opportunity to put the question until the meal was over and the men had joined the ladies in the drawing room. During a general buzz of conversation, he leaned towards her and told her in a low tone that so far all was well.

'Then they've consented to a betrothal?' she asked quietly.

He nodded. 'Had a bit of a raking down from Sir John, but he's agreed, provided I obtain my parents' consent. I've told Em, too, and she's promised to stand by me.'

'When are you going to break it to your parents?' asked Ginny.

'As soon as possible — tonight, if it can be managed. Em suggested I should inform Father, while she takes on the more tricky part of telling Mother. So if you see me leading Father off, you'll know what's happening, and just do your utmost to keep Frank away from us. Wish me luck, Ginny!'

She did, most sincerely, and soon afterwards he moved over to talk to Emmeline, leaving her to the vapidities of Lucilla. Presently she saw him in conversation with his father and after a few moments, they walked out of the room together.

'Mama,' said Emmeline, almost at once, 'I wish you will come up to my bedchamber for a moment. There is something I would particularly like you to see.'

Lady Turville, being comfortably settled far enough away from her niece to avoid the hazards of that young lady's conversation, at first demurred. But at last she yielded to her elder daughter's persistence, and they, too, went out, leaving the other three alone.

'What is all this?' demanded Frank, looking enquiringly at Ginny. 'I scent a mystery, and it wouldn't surprise me in the least to learn that you know all about it.'

'I can't think why you should say so,' she replied, trying to put on an innocent air.

'Doing it too brown, now, Ginny. I wonder what you've been up to, eh?'

Lucilla stifled a yawn with an elegant gesture. 'Evenings in the country are incredibly tedious,' she complained languidly. 'I feel quite worn out doing nothing, yet in Town one is always on the go without the slightest sign of fatigue.'

'Ah, but in London you are always surrounded by your faithful circle of admirers,' replied Frank, with a cynical smile. 'Admiration is the breath of life to you, dearest Lucy — without it, you are but a wilting plant, I fear.'

'And to be offensive is essential to *your* well-being, my dear brother,' she retorted, dispassionately. 'Since you are minded to practise your art — if such it can be called — I will leave you to exercise it on our cousin.'

So saying, she removed to the farthest corner of the room to occupy herself in riffling through the pages of some copies of the Ladies' Magazine.

'Now she has gone,' said Frank to Ginny, 'you need not scruple to unburden yourself. What is going on here tonight?'

'Well, I believe you'll discover soon enough, so perhaps there's no harm in telling you.'

She proceeded to unfold the story of Aubrey's love affair, keeping her voice low enough for it to escape Lucilla's ears. Frank heard her out for the most part in silence, now and then breaking into a laugh. Once he emitted a soft whistle which nevertheless earned him a disgusted glance from his sister.

'So he's been carrying on a clandestine affair all this time!' he exclaimed at the conclusion of her story. 'Aubrey, of all men! You must have had the deuce of a task to bring him up to scratch, Ginny — your powers of persuasion must be formidable! Do you know, I had quite the wrong impression? I was certain that you were the one he was after, and was almost ready to believe that you, too, were not averse to his attentions. I cannot tell you—' with a meaning look — 'how relieved I am to find myself mistaken.'

'Well, I should think so!' said Ginny, roundly. 'Aubrey and I — no, that would not do at all! I would be the worst kind of female for him. Miss Mandeville is admirably suited, on the other hand. She is gentle and yielding, and thinks of him as a tower of strength —'

Frank broke into another laugh.

'You are most unkind,' she informed him severely. 'Don't you see, that is the very thing he needs to put him on his mettle? Because *she* cannot take the initiative in anything, he will be obliged to do so. Depend upon it, she will be the making of Aubrey!'

'A Solomon come to judgment,' he mocked, but not unkindly. 'Perhaps you are right. But I doubt very much if Mother, at any rate, will sanction such a match. She is more concerned with the development of Aubrey's financial standing rather than his character.' He shook his head. 'No, Ginny, a sporting try on your part, but I fear you'll catch cold at it.'

'Well, we shall see,' replied Ginny, in an optimistic tone.

Meanwhile, her Aunt was finding it difficult to credit the news which Emmeline had just broken to her.

'But surely you must be mistaken?' she asked, amazed. 'Why, I am sure that he and Eugenia — only this morning I had occasion to reprove them for whispering together in the library, and they have been out driving together countless times lately!'

Not without some small signs of jealousy, for Aubrey had always been close to her in the old days, Emmeline explained that Eugenia had been helping him in the affair.

'Well, and if that isn't of a piece with her general conduct!' declared Lady Turville. 'I never encountered a more determined, self-opinionated girl in all my life! I can only be thankful that Aubrey has not fixed his interest with *her* — as I told you before, Emmeline, I don't think all her fortune could compensate for failings such as hers.'

'In that case, Mama, perhaps you wouldn't look unfavourably on a match with Henrietta Mandeville?'

Her mother hesitated. 'It is not what I'd hoped for,' she said, slowly. 'He could do a deal better for himself. Annabel Truscott, you know, has twenty thousand pounds, whereas the Mandevilles won't be able to furnish their daughter with more than a modest dowry. I think he should look about him a little longer before entering into a betrothal. After all, he is only three and twenty.'

Emmeline cast about in her mind for some telling argument to strengthen her case. 'But only think, Mama, since he and Eugenia have become so very confidential together over this affair, surely there's a danger that their intimacy may grow if Aubrey is not already betrothed to someone else? Many a match is made on the rebound, you know; and perhaps presently my brother may come to realise the advantages of a wealthy bride without pausing long enough to consider the drawbacks which even to you offset Eugenia's fortune.'

Lady Turville considered this. 'Well, there may be something in what you say,' she admitted. 'But after all, the wretched girl will only be here for less than a fortnight. Surely even Aubrey can contrive to rub through without making a fool of himself for that length of time?'

'Ah, but it isn't only a fortnight, Mama. Don't forget that afterwards they will both be in London, where they can meet as often as they choose since they are cousins, and Lady Milden could raise no possible objection. Moreover —' Emmeline thought this was a trump card — 'depend upon it, a disappointed lover always looks for a shoulder to cry on; and one thing I will say for my cousin Eugenia, is that she's very tender-hearted.'

Lady Turville felt all the force of this argument. 'Perhaps you are right, Emmeline. You have always understood Aubrey better than I, I must confess. Well, if his father raises no objection, I suppose I must let things be. I never had high hopes of Aubrey's making a brilliant match, so in a sense I suppose I'm not too disappointed. It's a respectable enough connection, after all, and he will have a bride whom at least he need not fear to introduce into Society. Yes, I dare say it will answer — but of course we must see what your father has to say.'

But Lord Turville was far more concerned with ascertaining the views of his wife on the matter. He greatly feared that he knew them already, and confessed as much to his highly nervous son, whose story he had just heard.

'As far as I'm concerned, no objection whatever, m'boy. Good family — hunted with Mandeville often enough, very good sort of man — pretty gal, little Henrietta, if I'm thinking of the right one. Fair hair, little doll look, that the gal? Only one thing —' he paused awkwardly — 'not much money, Y'know. Your Mother may not like it — demmed sure she won't, in fact. Got other notions for you, as perhaps you may know.'

Aubrey admitted this, but said that Emmeline was at that moment trying to persuade their mother to give her consent to the betrothal.

Lord Turville shook his head sceptically. 'Shouldn't think she'll manage it. Very difficult woman to persuade, your Mother — knows her own mind. Admirable, of course, but can be awkward sometimes. Em's not the one to do it — more hope with Lucy, but I dare say she wouldn't want to get involved —' Here he glanced at Aubrey, who shook his head. 'No, just so. Well,' he went on, more briskly, obviously wishing to conclude what he had found a trying interview, 'see how things go. If your Mother agrees, no reason why we shouldn't make you a more handsome allowance on your marriage. A house — horses, carriages — family, in time — no end of financial responsibilities to be met, I know.'

Aubrey broke into an eager acknowledgement of this unlooked for generosity on his father's part.

'No, no, only what I should do,' interrupted Lord Turville hastily. 'But if y'Mother dislikes the match, boy, not much I can do about it, I'm afraid. Do my best to support you, of course — goes without saying. But there's only one recipe for harmony in matrimony, take my word for it, and that's to let the females have their head. They will, anyway, in the end, so why argue? Only wastes good drinking time, eh?'

So saying, he winked knowledgeably, and Aubrey's audience was at an end.

Chapter XVI

But by the following day, everything had resolved itself happily for Aubrey, and long before it was time for the family to start for church, he was setting his curricle bowling along the road to Wendover, a song on his lips.

Lady Martyn and Sir Peter appeared together in the family pew, which looked much too large for them now that the last of their wedding party had returned home. Eugenia noticed that occasionally during the service Lucilla allowed her eyes to stray in that direction; but Sir Peter, with what might have been admirable restraint on his part, did not once glance towards the Turville pew.

After the service, the two families naturally came together, and Lady Martyn graciously accepted the invitation to dine with the Turvilles on the following evening.

'It is most kind,' she said. 'We are sadly quiet now that all our visitors are gone.'

'So I thought, and that is why I asked Peter if you would care to join us in a family dinner. There will be only the Mandevilles present besides ourselves. I dare say you are acquainted with them? I don't mean the whole family is coming,' Lady Turville added, with a smile. 'Just Sir John and his wife with their eldest daughter, Henrietta. They are by way of being particular friends of Aubrey's.'

She thought it politic at this stage to drop a small hint to their neighbours of events to come, and saw that both Sir Peter and his mother had grasped the implication. Sir Peter leaned confidentially towards Eugenia.

'Was this by any chance Aubrey's secret?' he asked her with a twinkle in his eye.

She nodded, then noticed Lucilla's slightly supercilious gaze on her and felt an unaccustomed surge of self-consciousness. Her eyes dropped shyly away from his and she turned quickly to address some trivial remarks to Francis. Sir Peter noticed the slight withdrawal, but could not account for it. He frowned, and fell into conversation with Lord Turville until the ladies were ready to return to their carriages. During the whole time that he had been standing with them, Eugenia noticed that never once had he either looked at or spoken to Lucilla, beyond the merest greeting when first they met. She would have liked to suppose this a good sign, but her knowledge of human behaviour went somewhat deeper than that. 'Don't touch fire if you don't want to be burnt,' Nancy had warned her in childhood. Was Peter Martyn obeying some such maxim at present? If so, then for him the enchantment could not yet be over. And what of Lucilla? But, puzzle over this as she might, Ginny could not breach the barrier of her cousin's inscrutability. Mere curiosity or even boredom with the service might have caused Lucilla to look about her in church; and the supercilious glance with which she had watched Ginny and Sir Peter in conversation was for her quite a normal type of facial expression.

Aubrey was absent for the whole day, a message to that effect having been brought by one of Sir John Mandeville's grooms.

'I dare say he'll be in no hurry to get back to Town now, what?' remarked his father, laughing. 'Expect we'll have him hanging about here for ever until the knot is tied.'

Lucilla, who had been informed of her brother's betrothal on the previous evening without betraying any particular surprise or even interest, now asked when the wedding was likely to be.

'Aubrey is anxious for it to take place as soon as possible,' replied Emmeline. 'Dear boy, he is so much in love! But something will depend upon the bride's parents, of course. They may feel that Henrietta should wait a little, as she is not yet eighteen.'

'Eighteen is a very good age at which to marry,' pronounced Lady Turville. 'I was not much older when I wed your Papa — and Lucilla was that age, too.'

'And do you feel, Lucy, that it's a good age for marriage?' asked Frank, with one of his mocking looks.

Lucilla shrugged. 'As good as any other, I suppose,' she replied indifferently. 'What is this girl like? I have never met her, of course.'

'You will do so tomorrow,' promised her mother. 'She and her parents are dining here with us.'

'But the Martyns are to come, are they not?'

'Yes, what difference does that make? I suppose you may still improve your acquaintance with Henrietta — that is, if Aubrey doesn't monopolise her in the tiresome way of engaged couples.'

Lucilla merely shrugged by way of a reply. But her mother understood her sufficiently well to see that she was placed next to Sir Peter when the party assembled round the dining table on Monday evening. Lady Turville was at one end of the table with Peter Martyn on her left and Sir John Mandeville on her right. She divided her conversation equally between them as a conscientious hostess should; so that in the intervals when she was not addressing Sir Peter, his choice lay between Lucilla on his left, or an awkwardly crossways conversation with

Emmeline and her husband, who were sitting together on Sir John Mandeville's other side.

Ginny was next to Frank at her uncle's end of the table and on the opposite side from Lucilla and Sir Peter, so that any conversation with them was impossible. Nevertheless, she had an excellent view of both did she choose to look that way; which for the most part she was careful not to do.

At first it seemed as if Peter Martyn had determined not to offer anything in the way of conversation to his attractive neighbour but the merest commonplaces, and even those were brief and infrequent. She suffered this for a time with her usual cool equanimity, answering briefly when addressed and not intruding any fresh subject herself. But presently she showed that she could take the initiative by asking him what were his future plans.

'Plans? I don't put myself to the effort of making any at present,' he answered, in a casual tone.

'But will you remain here at Misbourne House or will you take a house in Town?' she persisted, turning the full force of her compelling eyes upon him.

'It is too early for me to say — I am but just returned home, and there is a vast deal to be seen to about the estate.'

'But you have a good agent, have you not? Cooke — or some such name, if I recall aright. Or has he left your service?'

'No, he's still with me, and as reliable as ever. But even the best steward needs direction now and then and becomes disheartened if the owner shows no interest in what is done.'

She smiled, gently reproachful. 'You were always so conscientious, Peter. Most landowners are content to leave matters to their underlings. What is the saying? — One does not keep a dog and bark oneself.'

He glanced quickly at her, a spark of anger in his eyes.

'You're not much changed,' he said, before he could stop himself.

He had not intended to let their conversation take on either a personal or a reminiscent note; but she had been angling for just such a difference in tone, and felt tolerably pleased at her success.

'No — should I be?' she asked, ingenuously.

He made an impatient movement and looked down the table away from her. His glance came to rest on Ginny, who just then was regarding him gravely. She flashed him a quick smile before turning to address some light-hearted remark to Frank.

'Most people do change in four years,' he said.

'Have *you*, I wonder?'

He glanced at Ginny once more, but this time she was laughing with her neighbour. When he turned back to Lucilla, he was in command of himself again.

'I really can't say. Tell me, how do you go on with your Yorkshire cousin?'

If she was put out at the change of topic, she did not allow it to show. She gave a slight shrug.

'Well enough, though I fear we have little in common. She appears to be bookish.'

If she had hoped that this information might disgust him, she was to be disappointed.

'Indeed? Regrettably, our acquaintance hasn't reached the point where I could discover that. I find her a somewhat unusual young lady, though. Not just in the common way.'

'She wants a little Town polish, if that's what you mean. I understand she goes shortly to her godmother in London to acquire it.'

'Let us hope that she doesn't!' he exclaimed, impulsively.

She raised her fine eyebrows. 'Surely that is rather unkind?'

'I didn't mean it so. I meant only to say that I prefer her as she is — that it would be a pity for her to conform to a pattern.'

'I feel sure if she knew your views, she would do her utmost to oblige you,' said Lucilla, in a mocking tone. 'When may I wish you happy?'

He looked amused. 'How rapidly the female mind jumps to matchmaking! A man has only to express mild approval of some woman, and all his female acquaintances at once consider the pair as good as betrothed.'

'You understand us so well,' she returned, reassured by his answer. In her experience, which was considerable, a man rarely jested when his affections were seriously involved.

'Good God, I don't delude myself to that extent!'

'It's as well, perhaps.' Her eyes met his with a serious look. 'Believe me, we don't always understand ourselves.'

'That I can readily believe.'

Thinking this kind of talk dangerous, he turned to address some remark to Lady Turville, and prudently remained in conversation with her for several minutes. In the meantime Lucilla sat silent. Her other neighbour was Henrietta Mandeville, who was sitting next to Aubrey and therefore had scant attention to give to anyone else. Besides, she was more than a little in awe of the elegant Lady Ruscombe and would scarcely have ventured to speak first. Lucilla therefore occupied her time in glancing idly round the table; she found her eyes straying constantly to Eugenia as she turned over in her mind what Peter had said concerning her cousin.

Evidently his interest was caught in that quarter, even if not seriously. Nevertheless, it might be as well to make some small endeavour to discourage it. She waited until he was at liberty again, then smilingly directed his attention to where Eugenia and Frank were seated.

'They go on vastly well together, do you not think?' she asked.

His eyes followed hers. Ginny had flung back her head in laughter at some remark of Frank's; the curve of white throat and the sparkle in her expressive eyes somehow laid a constraint on Sir Peter's spirits.

'Yes, I suppose so.'

'Mama must be gratified,' continued Lucilla, ignoring his flat tone. 'She has been hoping that our cousin might make a match of it with one of my brothers. It looks very much as if she won't be disappointed.'

'Lady Turville has always been a talented matchmaker,' he replied drily.

She glanced warily at him, uncertain how to answer this. 'I suppose,' she said, after a pause, 'one might say the exercise of such talents could be considered part of a mother's duty towards her offspring.'

'To the extent of forcing them into a loveless marriage?' His tone was harsh.

'Ah, no!' she exclaimed, quickly. 'Not that — never that!'

Their eyes met briefly. Hers were dimmed with unshed tears, or so he believed for a moment. His look softened, and he stretched his hand out towards her, then moved it back again with an impatient gesture.

'You don't believe Frank to be indifferent to your cousin, then?' he asked.

His air and tone suggested that he was changing the subject rather than continuing with a previous one. She thought she understood him; he did not choose to mention what was uppermost in his mind at that moment.

'No, I don't think I do,' she replied, pretending to give some thought to this. 'Of course, she *is* an heiress, and any man who pays her attentions is bound to be considered by the world in general as a fortune hunter.'

He started a little. 'I'd never once considered Miss Eugenia's fortune — or, at least, not since I became acquainted with her. Wherever she goes, I think she would be valued for herself.'

'Very prettily said, Peter. And I think perhaps Frank is coming round to that opinion, though perhaps at first he may not have been quite as oblivious to her other, more material, attractions as you seem to have been. He is an original, my brother Francis; and as Cousin Eugenia may also lay claim to that title, they should deal very well together.'

'What of the lady? Do you think she reciprocates his interest?'

It was spoken casually; a sidelong glance failed to read anything significant in his expression. A passing interest, she thought, and now he sees that there is no point in pursuing it.

Aloud she said; 'I fear I am no authority on my cousin Eugenia's thoughts and emotions. I can only judge as one woman does of another, and what I see leads me to suppose her not indifferent to him.'

He glanced down the table again to Eugenia's smiling, animated face.

'I can only defer to your superior understanding of your own sex,' he said, with a twisted smile.

Chapter XVII

Ginny had certainly been finding her cousin Francis a most entertaining companion, in contrast to the gentleman on her other side, who was Emmeline's husband Joseph Welwyn. As Mr. Welwyn was sitting beside his wife and they seemed totally absorbed in a private, domestic conversation, the few remarks he did address to Eugenia were civil commonplaces which required little thought or interest in answering. She turned to Frank with relief, and he laid himself out to please her, using his ready wit to advantage. Nevertheless, it did not escape his notice that on one or two occasions she glanced briefly across the table to where Lucilla and Sir Peter were sitting side by side. It had crossed his mind before that his young cousin from Yorkshire showed signs of developing an interest in Peter Martyn, but the notion did not disturb him unduly. After all, the girl had met Martyn only a few times; whereas he, Frank, was under the same roof with her and able to devote all his time to her, did he so wish. And he did wish it, suddenly, quite strongly, and not for that fabulous fortune, either. Miss Eugenia Turville was a prize worth possessing on her own account, and damned if he would not make a push to engage her interest. The slight element of rivalry involved only gave the affair a bit more of a sporting turn. He felt reasonably secure of success. He was no coxcomb, but he knew himself to be not unattractive to the fair sex when he chose to exert himself to please. Anyway, if he knew anything of his sister Lucilla, she was after Peter Martyn herself. And when Lucilla was on the trail, no other female stood a chance. Certainly not an eighteen-year-old girl who, however lively and fascinating she might be, could not possibly have the experience to out-manoeuvre a seasoned campaigner such as his sister; moreover, there was that old attachment between the two to be taken into account.

It might have surprised him a little to know that Ginny's reflections when she was watching Lucilla and Sir Peter were much the same as his own. She had the misfortune to glance their way on the occasion when Sir Peter had seemed about to take Lucilla's hand, then had drawn back. Such a gesture could only mean that he still loved Lucilla, thought Ginny; after that, she did not look their way again, but gave all her attention to her cousin, becoming even more animated than before.

The meal being over, the ladies removed to the drawing room while the gentlemen sat over their wine. Lady Martyn motioned to Ginny to come and sit beside her on a striped satin sofa; Ginny obeyed the smiling summons readily, for she had taken an instant liking to Sir Peter's mother. They chatted easily of this and that, but it soon appeared to Ginny that Lady Martyn was at some pains to find out something about her tastes and interests.

At last, the older woman gave a small sigh. 'Do you know,' she said, 'talking to you, Miss Turville, has made me realise how much I'm going to miss Eleanor? It's a very comfortable thing to have a young daughter about the house — it livens one up prodigiously! Not, of course, that one would wish to keep the poor dears unmarried for that very purpose,' she added, with a touch of her son's dry humour. 'Such an enterprise would be self-defeating, don't you think? One would end up by living with a desiccated old maid, most likely.'

Ginny laughed in acknowledgement of this, then said, 'You don't find a son answers the same purpose, ma'am?'

'Oh, no, not the *same* purpose. Sons are quite another kind of requirement — a man about the house, you know. Useful in case of trouble of various kinds, for such matters as keeping one's cook up to the mark and for overseeing the estate.'

Ginny laughed again. 'You're humbugging me, Lady Martyn! I refuse to believe that this is all the value you set on your son!'

'Oh, no, I said no such thing, now did I? If you will have the truth, my dear Miss Turville —' she lowered her voice to a conspiratorial level, causing Lucilla to look towards her sharply — 'I am hard put to it to preserve a decent reticence where praise of Sir Peter is concerned. I am constantly reminding myself that on no account must I fall into the error of playing The Fond Mama. Not to speak of earning that gentleman's most severe disapproval, if I should err in his hearing. Now you have my secret, and I trust you will honour it.'

Ginny schooled herself to present a grave face as she promised.

'But the point I was making — should it not be too far out of sight for you to have retained the slightest interest in it — was that a mother can enjoy all kinds of little feminine chats with a daughter, which would be completely boring to a son. Not only fashions, whether one will wear the lilac or the blue or purchase something new instead; but all those intimate little cosies about family or friends, which gentlemen so unfairly stigmatize as gossip. Real gossip is malicious, wouldn't you say?' Ginny nodded. 'But what I have in mind is kindly meant, and often helpful. Although,' she added, fairly, 'Peter may be right when he says that these are exercises in self-indulgence, and may sometimes do more harm than good.'

'One needs a little self-indulgence now and then,' said Ginny, 'if one's not to become a prig. But we don't believe in too much of it where I come from, ma'am.'

'Do tell me about your home, Miss Turville — may I say Miss Eugenia? There is something very stiff about the former mode of address, which does not fit your personality at all.'

'You may call me Ginny, ma'am, if you will, for that's always been my name at home, and I miss hearing it — except that I've lately persuaded my cousins Aubrey and Frank to make use of it. I don't think, though,' she added, glancing at Lady Turville, who was holding a surprisingly animated conversation with Hetty and her mother, 'that my Aunt really approves.'

'Fortunately I am not obliged to consult your Aunt's wishes in such a matter, as she is not your guardian,' replied Lady Martyn, in quite a different tone from any she had used hitherto. 'Yes, Ginny, by all means — perhaps Miss Ginny when others are by. We shall see. But pray tell me about your home. You are an orphan, I believe — that is so sad, poor child.'

'One becomes accustomed,' said Ginny, stoically. 'My mother died before I was three years old, so I cannot remember her. I was looked after in infancy by Nancy, who came to my mother before my birth, and is still with me as my personal maid. My godmother, Lady Milden, took a very maternal interest in me, helping Papa in the matter of choosing a suitable governess and later a school. She has no daughter of her own, and we are very close — quite like the best kind of aunt and niece relationship. And Papa was there some of the time, to joke me and take me riding, and provide all kinds of little treats.' She sobered. 'I missed him very much when he died eight years ago. Afterwards, Lord and Lady Milden were kinder than ever to me. I used to spend some part of my holidays from the seminary with them, and the remainder with Granpa Ackroyd.'

She spoke this name with a mixture of warmth and pride that at once caught the older woman's attention.

'Ah, yes, your mother's father. I collect you are very fond of the old gentleman?'

'He would not lay claim to such a title,' said Ginny, candidly. 'He's a plain Yorkshireman, ma'am, and as proud as they come. And I, too, feel proud of being his granddaughter.'

She looked at Lady Martyn in a challenging way as she said this. The older woman patted her hand approvingly.

'And so you may be, Ginny. My son tells me that the world is changing, and that the nation's manufacturers will before long carve out a new path of prosperity for us. The signs are there, he says, for those who have the perception to read them.'

'I see, ma'am, that your son has many other uses for you than those you outlined just now,' replied Ginny, on a lighter note.

All the same, she was pleased by Lady Martyn's remark. If Sir Peter thought in this way, he would surely not join her relatives in despising Granpa Ackroyd for his vulgar Trade connections? And then she asked herself what difference it could make whatever he thought on the subject. He was not remotely interested in anything concerning Eugenia Turville.

Their conversation was interrupted at this point by the gentlemen coming into the room. Sir Peter, after one quick glance around, came to join his mother and Ginny. Lucilla had looked up briefly, but she now turned away and seemed to be absorbed in what her mother was discussing with Lady Mandeville and Hetty.

'Ginny and I have been enjoying a very comfortable little chat together,' Lady Martyn greeted her son. 'We've agreed on the value of a young woman's presence in the home to liven up elderly dowagers; and had you not come in so soon, I hoped to have been able to persuade her to look in on me occasionally when she happens to be passing. Quite informally, you know,' she added to Ginny.

Sir Peter raised his eyebrows a trifle at hearing Eugenia's pet name used, but nodded and said he considered this a very good notion.

'And in case you shouldn't chance to be passing for some time,' he amended with a smile, 'could we not name a day not too far ahead — say tomorrow, for instance?'

'Why, yes, an excellent suggestion!' Lady Martyn seconded him, swiftly. 'Now which would you prefer, my dear, morning or afternoon?'

Ginny, stifling a sudden wild impulse to agree to both, replied that either would suit very well. 'But of course I must ask my Aunt,' she added, reluctantly.

'Of course; but I will do that for you. Perhaps you had best come in the morning, and then if you do not tire of us too quickly, we can perhaps persuade you to stay on into the afternoon. What do you say? It might amuse you to see over the house and grounds.'

'Though I fear we cannot promise you any antiquarian delights,' put in Sir Peter. 'The house is no more than sixty years old.'

'What, no cloisters or crumbling towers?' demanded Ginny, with a pout. 'No secret passages or priests' holes? Well, I must say I think that's shabby!'

All three laughed; and Frank, whose attention had been caught by Ginny's nonsensical remark, joined in, too.

'Well, if Mrs. Radcliffe's to your taste, Cousin Ginny,' he said, 'we can oblige you here, for you must know that we still have a secret passage — and there may even be a skeleton or two mouldering in it by now, with any luck!'

Lady Turville looked up from her conversation. 'I beg you won't start any nonsense of that kind, Francis! We had enough trouble over that wretched passage when you and Aubrey were boys, and that is why we had the exit sealed off. And even that did not completely discourage you from playing there — I recall on one occasion Aubrey was shut in for several hours, and no one could think where he was. Or at least,' she added, looking hard at Frank, 'no one *admitted* to having the least notion, but it was you who finally suggested we should look there.'

'Eh, what's that?' asked Lord Turville, who was talking to Hetty's father, but had overheard this reminiscence. 'That time Aubrey got himself shut in the hidey-hole? No doubt about who was responsible, my dear Sophia — but no evidence, so the only thing was to tan 'em both. Still, they won't either of 'em thank us for bringing that up,' he added, tardily.

'No, b'God!' muttered Aubrey, too low for his beloved to hear.

Frank, however, merely looked amused and glanced at his sister Lucilla, who had not been talking herself, but listening idly to Ginny's conversation with the Martyns. She met his quizzical look with a bland stare.

'Oh, but that's famous!' exclaimed Ginny her eyes lighting up. 'Not about Aubrey being locked in, I don't mean, but that you actually have a secret passage on the premises. Do, pray do, show it to me!'

'If you must see it, Eugenia,' said her Aunt in repressive accents, 'Francis can show it to you at some more suitable time. I am sure none of our guests would have the slightest interest in peering into what is no more than a dark — and, I fear, exceedingly dirty — hole.'

'No, of course not,' replied Ginny, swallowing her chagrin at this public reproof, especially in front of Sir Peter and his mother. 'I only meant that I'd like to see it at some time.'

'Well, so you shall,' Frank reassured her. 'Tomorrow, give you my word.'

'That will be splendid, Frank, but I'm promised to Lady Martyn for tomorrow.'

Frank raised his eyebrows.

'If you'll be good enough to state a convenient time,' put in Sir Peter, quickly, 'I shall do myself the honour of fetching you.'

'Oh, but there's no occasion for me to put you to so much trouble, sir!' she protested. 'You are very good, but it's no distance — I can easily ride.'

'By all means, then we may ride together. At what hour shall I come for you?'

After a little discussion, they fixed on eleven o'clock.

'Is there such an hour?' quizzed Frank.

'Not in London, certainly,' agreed Sir Peter, with a grin. 'But we rustics in our rural retreat, you know, dear boy —'

'Are up to every rig and row — you don't need to tell me that,' retorted Frank, meaningly. 'Some rustic, you, Martyn!'

They looked at each other for a moment in an amused, measuring kind of way which did not entirely escape either Ginny's or Lucilla's notice. Lady Martyn, too, was watching quietly.

At this point, Lady Turville cut across everyone else's conversations with what she evidently considered an important announcement.

'I am sure you will all be interested to hear what Lady Mandeville and I have been discussing. It seems that she and Sir John intend to arrange a ball for next week at the Red Lion to mark the occasion of their daughter's eighteenth birthday. We are agreed that it would be a most suitable time at which to announce Henrietta's betrothal to Aubrey. Do you not think so, Sir John?' She turned to her husband. 'And you, my dear?'

Of course both gentlemen agreed; and the subject of the forthcoming ball occupied most of the ladies present for what remained of the evening.

Chapter XVIII

Ginny went to bed in a nervous flutter of spirits for which she could not entirely account. She was to visit a rather pleasant middle-aged lady on the following day, and there was nothing very remarkable in that. It was the kind of mild social occasion which was well within her scope. Could it be because she was to be escorted to that meeting by a gentleman whom she had met for the first time less than a fortnight ago, and on infrequent, sometimes unconventional occasions since? Surely she was not such a sentimental ninny, she asked herself severely, as to imagine either that she was in love with him or that he had any interest in her? She shook her head vigorously, as though to brush off any such foolish thoughts. All the same, she rather feared that indeed she was. And then she recalled how he had looked at Lucilla when they were seated together at the dining table; the picture came back so clearly to her mind, it might almost have been printed there. It was hardly surprising that sleep did not come to her very readily that night.

She arose in the same unsettled frame of mind. When Nancy asked her which riding dress she would wear, she at first requested the green one, then reconsidered this decision in favour of a plum-coloured habit with a black velvet collar and black frogged fastenings. Nancy obediently laid this out, but Ginny looked at it doubtfully.

'I don't know,' she said, hesitating. 'It's very nice, of course, but perhaps the green — oh, what do you think, Nancy?'

'What I think is your wits are woolgathering, Miss Ginny!' exclaimed the abigail. 'First you want the green, then it's the red, now it's the green again — ha' done, do, for pity's sake, lass! Wear, this, and he can't help but admire you.'

'Nancy!' Ginny rounded on her with a haughty look that sat very ill on her good-tempered face. 'How dare you presume so!'

'Nay, love, I meant no offence, as you well know. But a body can't but draw her own conclusions when you're all of a fidget over a morning call! Which is summat I never did see with you before, even when you was just out of the nursery. Still, pardon me if I spoke too free.'

Ginny flung her arms around Nancy's ample form. 'No, pardon *me*, dear Nan! Yes, I am in a fidget and I know it's foolish, and I'm cross with myself, not you.'

'As if I didn't know that,' replied the maid, holding the dress for her mistress to step into. 'There's no explanations needed, Miss Ginny, 'twixt thee and me. All the same,' she finished, having done up all the fastenings and stepped back to cast a critical eye over her young mistress, 'yon dress looks a treat, and no mistake.'

Looking at herself in the long mirror, Ginny was inclined to agree. The dark red of the habit showed her creamy skin and brown curls to advantage, and its fit was perfect. She swept her skirts about her with a touch of bravado, and took her way downstairs to breakfast.

Here she found four members of the family already seated, her Aunt and Uncle with Emmeline and Joseph Welwyn. The Welwyns were to return home today as soon as breakfast was over. Aubrey and Lucilla presented themselves soon after Eugenia sat down, but of Frank there was no sign as yet. There was little conversation; Lord Turville was occupied with his newspaper, Aubrey was bolting his food in order to get on the road to Wendover as soon as possible, while a morning languor seemed to envelop the others. Lost in her own thoughts, Ginny did not mind sitting silently through the meal. After it was over, the Welwyns' carriage was brought round to the door, farewells were spoken, and the couple drove off without a backward glance. Aubrey left soon afterwards, Lord and Lady Turville disappeared on their own separate concerns, leaving Lucilla and Ginny in the morning room to the enjoyment of a tête-à-tête, had they so wished. But for once Ginny was disinclined for conversation; as Lucilla rarely took the initiative in such matters, the two continued to sit in silence.

After about twenty minutes of this, Frank entered the room looking jovially around.

'Oh, there you are, Ginny. Good morning — and good morning to you, Lucy. What's amiss? Never saw such a lot of Friday faces — missing Em and that lively husband of hers? They do leave a gap in the family circle, what?'

'There are others whose absence would be a decided advantage,' retorted Lucilla coldly.

'Agreed — but doubtless we wouldn't agree on names,' he replied airily, lifting a dish cover on the sideboard and inspecting the contents. 'Well, Ginny, if you can contain your love of the Gothic until such time as I've consumed a slice or two of ham, I'll lead you to the secret passage we were talking of last night.'

Ginny brightened at once. 'Oh, would you? I should like that of all things, but —' she glanced at her watch doubtfully — 'Will there be time, do you suppose? Sir Peter is to call for me at eleven.'

'And it's now barely a quarter after ten. How long will it take, do you suppose? We have but to step into the library, press a concealed catch and hey presto! the passage is revealed. We shall need a candle, of course, for you to see its full Gothic splendour — and also to avoid falling down the steps. There'll be one to hand.'

The suggestion appealed strongly to Ginny. She had been wondering what she could do to kill time until Sir Peter was due to call for her; she felt disinclined to settle to anything, yet was in too much of a fidget to sit still. She emulated Lucilla's example by picking up one from a pile of copies of the Ladies' Magazine, and pretended to be looking at it.

Presently Frank pushed back his chair and announced himself ready to start. She glanced at her watch again; it was only half past ten. Lucilla did not look up as Ginny rose from her seat and followed Frank out of the room. They met no one as they crossed the hall to the library, shutting the door behind them. Frank took a candle from one of the stands and lit it, holding it aloft in his left hand.

'Now!' he said, in a whisper charged with mystery. 'Come over here, and I will reveal the secret lock!'

She moved obediently to a panelled section of the wall by which he was standing.

'This is called linenfold panelling, as perhaps you may know.' She nodded. 'Yes, well, we lift this, so —'

He raised a section of the folded design, revealing underneath a small metal knob fitted into a plate, all of which lay neatly below the linenfold when it was in place.

'No one who didn't know would ever guess it was there, would they?' he asked, still in a mysterious undertone.

'No, indeed!' She found herself catching the infection of his manner. 'How very ingenious! And does one turn the knob to open the door to the secret passage?'

'Ordinarily, yes, but there's a safety lock fitted which operates on this side only by the simple expedient of pushing the knob in. As this place has been kept locked for years, we will now need first to pull out the knob before turning it. The idea was, you see, that anyone using the passage could be prevented from bursting out of it unawares into the midst of enemies. A friend in this room who knew the mechanism could lock the door so that the man in hiding could not open it from his side.'

'And the friend would release it again when all was safe,' finished Ginny, in an excited tone. 'Oh, how romantic it all is!'

'Not so very romantic, if a man should be fleeing for his life,' Frank replied. 'But looking back in these less troubled times, yes, perhaps so. Shall we open it now?'

'Oh, yes, please!'

He pulled out the knob and tried to turn it, but experienced some difficulty at first.

'It's an age since we used it,' he said, flexing his fingers and trying again. 'It's deuced stiff, confound it — ah, that's it!'

There was a slight click, and suddenly a whole section of the panelling swung back in the manner of a door, revealing what looked like a cupboard behind.

'Come,' invited Frank, and holding the candle aloft, took her hand and drew her inside.

The door swung to behind them. Ginny gave a little cry of alarm, but he reassured her quickly.

'It's all right — see, there's a knob on this side, too, and we can open it easily. It's only when it's locked on the other side that one can't turn it. Look, how do you like it? Isn't it splendidly ghoulish and mysterious?'

He held the candle aloft, inviting her to share in his excursion into the remembered pleasures of boyhood. For a moment she looked at his face, rather than at the secret room he had brought her to see. He appeared different now, as if he had shed the cynical, devil-may-care façade which the world knew as the Honourable Francis Turville, and had become the man whom the boy might have made, in different circumstances.

She turned to look at the room, shuddering as a cobweb brushed across her face. It was — not unexpectedly — festooned with cobwebs, and was about five feet square, only just large enough to accommodate them both. Careless of his coat, he swept the cobwebs from around her with a wide gesture of his arm, then directed her attention to a narrow door set in the back wall.

'Look, Ginny — the way to the passage!'

He swung back the door, holding the candle to reveal a flight of steps and a dark tunnel beyond.

'It's not very long, and it used to come out in one of the cellars, but my parents blocked it off, as you heard yesterday evening. Aubrey and I used to have famous fun here before that, with some of our playfellows — Peter Martyn among them.' He paused, gazing down the stairs. 'Still, no point in taking you down — you've seen the exciting bit, and it's bound to be dirty down there. You'll want to brush your gown before you go visiting, I dare say. Come along, then, if you've looked your fill. I'm sorry about the skeletons — perhaps we'll find them another day.'

'Pray don't exert yourself for me,' laughed Ginny. 'I can go on very well without them. But it's been most exciting, Frank — I wouldn't have missed seeing it for worlds!'

'Capital,' he replied, somewhat absently, as he shut the door leading to the stairs, and turned towards the one by which they had entered. 'It's one advantage of living in a house that goes back to the Dark Ages.'

'Well, not quite the Dark Ages,' objected Ginny, with a passion for accuracy, 'but never mind that.'

Frank did not answer her. He had found the knob on the exit door, but was having difficulty turning it.

'Here, hold the candle, Ginny, while I have another go at this confounded thing.'

She obeyed, holding the candle aloft so that he would have enough light to see what he was doing.

'Deuced odd,' he muttered, after a few minutes spent in twisting the doorknob one way and another. 'It turns readily enough, which is all that's needed to open the devilish contraption! I can't understand it, unless — no, that couldn't be it, though — who would do such a damnable thing?'

'Couldn't be what?' she asked, sharply. 'What do you mean?'

He made no answer for a moment, then turned a grim face towards her.

'It is though, b'God! Some confounded idiot has locked us in here, Ginny!'

Chapter XIX

'Oh, no! Are you positive it won't open?' demanded Ginny, alarmed. 'Here, let me try for a moment.'

'By all means.'

He took the candle from her and stepped aside so that she could reach the knob. She turned it this way and that for a time, but at last was obliged to admit defeat.

'Are you sure that it isn't just stuck in some way, Frank? After all, you did say that it's many years since it was used. Do, pray, try again! I shall be late for my appointment with Sir Peter, and that would appear so uncivil!'

He made no answer, but seized the knob and did his best to make it work.

'The devilish thing turns easily enough, Ginny, and I assure you that's all it needs to open the door. I've done it often enough in the past. No, the plain fact is that somebody must have locked it from the other side.'

'But why? Who would do such a thing?'

'Almost anyone who came into the library and found that section of panelling turned back revealing the lock. Most of the servants and all the family know of the existence of this hidey hole, and also that it's always kept locked. No one would ever think of somebody being inside, I dare say — it would be natural to close it up again.'

'But we haven't been in here much more than five minutes,' objected Ginny, 'and there was no one about when we came into the library. Besides, wouldn't anyone in there have heard our voices through the wall?'

Frank shook his head. 'You may remember that we were speaking very low. Besides, I know from past experience that one needs to shout at full volume before being heard in the library.'

'Well, we'd best start doing that now,' said Ginny, forcefully, 'unless we want to spend the rest of the morning in here. That, is, if you don't know of any other way out.'

''Fraid not, since the exit to the passage was blocked up. I might be able to force the lock with a suitable tool, of course, but the devil of it is that I haven't so much as a penknife about me. I've been searching my pockets.'

'I suppose a hairpin's no good? I've some of those, of course, if I unfasten my hair.'

'Not strong enough. No, there's nothing for it but to yell until someone hears us. Devilish infra dig, what? And if there's no one in the room at present, it might take some time before we attract attention.'

'Oh, I do hope not!' exclaimed Ginny in dismay. 'What time is it now? Ten minutes to eleven? Oh, dear, we must make them hear at once — pray shout for all you're worth, Frank, and so will I!'

He obediently emitted a loud hunting cry that almost deafened his companion. After a moment she added her voice to his, producing a clamour that caused them considerable discomfort in such a small, enclosed space. They kept this up for several minutes, then paused.

'Must have a breather,' panted Frank. 'Try banging on the wall for a while.'

Doubling up his fists, he attacked the door aggressively, then stopped to listen.

'Can't hear a sound,' he said, at last. 'Hate to say so, but I fear there's no one in the room at present. Whoever locked the door must have left immediately afterwards. Still, if we keep up this din, someone's bound to hear a faint echo of it in the hall. I should have thought, and will come into the library to investigate. Nothing else for it, Ginny — sorry. We'll have to yell once more.'

They raised their voices in unharmonious unison.

Shortly before eleven o'clock Sir Peter rode up to the door of Lydeard Hall and was shown into the morning room, where Lucilla was sitting with her mother. He was greeted affably by Lady Turville, who presently recalled that he had come to call for Eugenia and despatched a servant to the latter's room to inform her that Sir Peter was waiting.

After an interval, the messenger returned to say that Miss Eugenia was not in her room.

'Her maid tells me, milady, that she hasn't set eyes on her mistress at all since she came down to breakfast.'

'Tut, tut!' Lady Turville shook her head in disapproval as she dismissed the servant. 'Now where in the world can the tiresome girl have gone? Do you know, Lucilla?'

'I, Mama?' Lucilla raised surprised eyebrows. 'Why should you suppose so?'

'Well, I did leave you sitting here with your cousin when I went off to speak to the housekeeper,' replied her mother. 'I thought perhaps she might have mentioned what she intended to do.'

'Conversation is always at a low ebb during breakfast, don't you think?' Lucilla turned to Sir Peter for corroboration, and he nodded. 'Besides,' she added, 'I was looking at a magazine, you know, and not paying particular attention to either Frank or Eugenia.'

'Pray don't worry on my account,' said Sir Peter. 'I have no pressing engagements this morning and can very well await Miss Eugenia's pleasure.'

Accordingly they all three fell into conversation again, until presently Lady Turville excused herself, saying there was some domestic matter requiring her attention.

Sir Peter glanced at the clock. It was now nearly half past eleven.

'I fear I may be taking up too much of your time,' he said to Lucilla, apologetically.

'Not at all. I have nothing in the world to do here, you know, and, anyway, it is so pleasant to sit and chat like this. Quite like old times, don't you agree, Peter?'

He assented, but with a constraint in his manner that suggested he was not quite at his ease.

Lucilla glanced ostentatiously at the clock. 'It appears very much as if my cousin has quite overlooked her arrangement with you.'

'Yes, I fear it does,' he answered shortly.

'Of course, she is very young and rather naïve, and her attention may easily wander from one thing to another.'

'That is not at all how I read her character.'

'Oh?' Lucilla gave her sweetest smile. 'Pray tell me what you make of her, for I must admit she has me in something of a puzzle.'

'I cannot think why,' he replied, quietly. 'It seems to me that Miss Eugenia is a very straightforward kind of young lady, who would leave no one in any doubt either of her opinions or her intentions.'

'And you find this admirable, no doubt?' Her tone was light, almost teasing.

'I find it different, at any rate, from what one is accustomed to with ladies.'

'Ah, but then some females study to be different in order to appear more interesting.'

He gave an austere smile. 'No man who has been about a little can be totally unaware of that. Nevertheless, I venture to think that Miss Eugenia's conduct in general owes little to art.'

'No, perhaps not,' she said, thoughtfully. 'I remember thinking when I was first introduced to her a few days ago that she was a child of Nature. But do tell me, Peter, —' with a change of tone — 'why is it we always seem to discuss my cousin, you and I, whenever we chance to find ourselves together?'

He paused for a moment, then decided to accept her challenge.

'Possibly,' he replied, fixing her with a long, steady regard, 'because there are so many other topics we cannot discuss,'

'Ah!' Her breath came out in a fluttering sigh. 'But are you quite sure, Peter, that we cannot?'

His expression hardened. 'Nothing can be more certain.'

She stretched out an appealing hand towards him. 'Ah, Peter, you are so — unforgiving! Can you not try to understand?'

He ignored her outstretched hand.

'I believe I understand very well, though it has taken me some years to do so.'

'Oh, you mean something horridly cynical by that, I am sure, but if only I had ever had the chance to explain it all to you, I know you would feel differently!'

Her voice was no longer cool and detached now, but warmed by an emotion that was reflected in those usually calm, clear blue eyes. In spite of himself, his pulse beat more strongly in response.

At that unpropitious moment, Lady Turville burst into the room.

'Goodness gracious, is my niece not here yet? Really, it's passing all the bounds of civility to keep you waiting for her in this way — three quarters of an hour late, and no message left, or anything! Just wait until I set eyes on Miss Eugenia, and I promise you she shall have a piece of my mind!'

'I beg you won't mention it, ma'am. It's of no account,' said Sir Peter, quickly recovering his composure after the interruption. 'All the same, it does appear that our arrangement may have slipped your niece's mind, and that being so, I must not trespass any further on your time.'

'Now I come to think of it, Mama,' put in Lucilla, 'I believe I did partly hear Frank and my cousin discussing some expedition or other over breakfast — only as I told you, I wasn't really attending to them so I've no notion what it may have been. And they did leave the parlour together shortly afterwards.'

'Well!' exploded her mother. 'Words fail me!'

Lucilla glanced covertly at Sir Peter to see how he had taken her information, but his face was once more schooled to polite inscrutability. He rose to take his leave, civilly refusing all offers of refreshment.

'Would you be so very good, ma'am, as to inform Miss Eugenia when she returns that my mother will be delighted to see her at any time? If today was not convenient, after all, that doesn't signify in the least. Your servant, ma'am — Lucy.'

He bowed and left them to their own reflections. Lady Turville continued to pursue hers out aloud for some time, but Lucilla was very much more restrained.

After a time, they were interrupted by Lord Turville, who strode into the room as though a trifle out of temper.

'Either of you seen Frank?' he demanded. 'No sign of him out of doors, and his valet says he came down to breakfast just after ten. I've been hanging around the stables waiting for him to turn up — we'd planned to be off to Aylesbury together at eleven. These cubs are all the same — demmed unpunctual! Though I must say Frank don't as a rule let me down in that way. Know where he is, either of you?'

'No, but I would give much to know,' retorted his wife, grimly. 'As far as I can conjecture, he seems to have gone off with Eugenia, for she, too, is missing. The height of rudeness to Peter Martyn, who's been awaiting her this hour or more — but there! it's all of a piece with the rest of her conduct! I wish the tiresome girl had never entered our house!'

'Gone off with Eugenia?' repeated Lord Turville. 'You don't mean to say the two of 'em have eloped, eh, Sophie? No, damme, if that's not too much!'

'Don't be so feather-brained, my dear. Of course I don't suppose they've eloped! Why on earth should they do so? If they wish to marry, I dare say no one will throw the slightest rub in the way — though I, for one,' she added, 'cannot pretend that I would be overjoyed to have Eugenia for a daughter. No, it's not so bad as that. But they are both missing, and by what Lucilla tells me, it seems that they have gone out together somewhere.'

Her husband shook his head. 'He wouldn't do it — no, damme, the boy's a bit of a care-for-nobody, but I never yet knew him let me down when he'd undertaken to be there. Lucy must be mistaken.'

Lucilla shrugged. 'Well, I may be, Papa. I wasn't really attending to their conversation, but I thought I heard them planning something together this morning.'

'At breakfast, was it?' She nodded. 'Yes, well then, it must have been something Frank expected to be finished with by eleven. Must've been held up in some way — devilish annoying!'

'You don't think,' began Lady Turville, with a hint of uneasiness, 'that they could have had some kind of mishap — an accident? Oh, goodness, what in the world will I say to Lady Milden if Eugenia has come to any harm? She will be certain to think I should have looked after the girl better!'

Lord Turville reflected for a moment. 'Shouldn't think much harm could come to her with Frank there. Well up to snuff, that boy — bruising rider, good shot, handy pair of fives —'

His wife gave a little cry of alarm. 'Oh, heavens, never say you think they've been set on by footpads! But, no, it's ridiculous in broad daylight, and in our own countryside, too! Now you've succeeded in making me uneasy, we'd best look for them — instruct the servants to search the house and grounds first, and then we must think what is to be done afterwards, if they cannot be found!'

'If you are to go searching for them,' said Lucilla, who had listened to this interchange with a faintly uneasy expression, 'why don't you look in the library first?'

Her father stared at her. 'The library? What the devil would a fellow like Frank be doing in the library at this time of day? Damme, it isn't even raining!'

'It's just a notion I had,' replied Lucilla, with rather less than her usual assurance. 'I'm not certain, but I may have heard Frank mention something to my cousin concerning the library.'

'The library!' exclaimed her mother, triumphantly. 'Then I have it! You remember all that stupid talk last night about the secret room, and how Eugenia declared she must see it?

Depend upon it, Frank has taken her there, and they must have got locked in, or something of the kind.'

Lord Turville slapped his thigh. 'Ten to one you're right, my love! Come on, let's see!'

Leading the way from the parlour and down the hall, he flung open the door of the library. Immediately a muffled sound of thumping came to his ears. With a muttered curse, he crossed to the panelling which concealed the secret door, closely followed by his wife and daughter. In a few seconds, he had moved back the panel to reveal the lock.

'Just as you thought, wife! They're inside, and some fool has turned the lock on 'em.' He raised his voice. 'Hang on, Frank, we'll have got you out in a trice!'

He unfastened the door. It swung open, and two dishevelled figures staggered out.

'How long have you been in there?' demanded Lord Turville, aghast.

'Too devilish long by half!' returned Frank. 'What wouldn't I give for a pint of ale at this moment! I'm sorry to have kept you waiting, Father, but you can see it was no fault of mine. Only thought to take a few minutes after breakfast to show Ginny this place, and curse it, if some fool doesn't go and turn the lock on us! We've been yelling our heads off and banging away ever since.' He turned to Eugenia, whom he was still supporting with one arm. 'You all right, Ginny?'

Ginny looked far from all right. Her hair was hanging down her back in disarray, her face was pale, and her riding habit covered in dust and cobwebs. But she smiled wanly.

'I shall feel more the thing in a few moments — a trifle out of breath, that's all.' She paused, gulped, then added anxiously, 'Sir Peter? Did he come — is he still waiting?'

'To be sure he came, but you can scarce expect that he would wait all this time,' replied her Aunt, severely. 'To be getting up to such tricks is most unseemly, Eugenia. You'd best go up to your room and lie down for a while to recover.'

'But what must he have thought? Did he seem vexed?' panted Ginny, trying to push back her hair from her face.

'He seemed not at all put out. He concluded that you must have forgotten about your arrangement for this morning, and bade me tell you that Lady Martyn would be pleased to see you at any other time.'

'Oh, dear!' Her voice trembled, and she was obviously very close to tears.

Frank patted her hand reassuringly. 'Never trouble your head over what the Martyns may think — they'll understand right enough when they learn what happened. But m'mother's right, Ginny, you should go and rest now. Lucy, take her up to her room.'

This forced Lucilla to come forward and offer her arm to her cousin, though she did so with obvious reluctance.

Eugenia shook her head. 'No, thank you, Cousin, I shall do very well on my own. Nancy will be there. But I must go over to Misbourne House as soon as possible to explain.'

'I'll go for you,' offered Frank, 'once I've quenched my thirst.'

'No, I must go myself,' she said forcefully.

'Very well, if you insist, then I'll accompany you,' said Frank, in a commanding tone. 'But later, Ginny, when you've had time to recover. Pray go up to your abigail now, and let her make you comfortable, do.'

'Yes, child,' agreed Lord Turville, 'nasty experience for a young female, b'God, and you might well take harm of it if you don't have a care. Good thing Lucy suggested looking first in the library, or we might have wasted another hour or so before we ran you to earth, eh?'

'Oh, so Lucy suggested coming into the library!' asked Francis, giving his sister a searching look. 'I wonder why she thought of that?'

Lucilla's eyes slid away from his. 'Just a notion I had,' she said, with a shrug.

'A surprising accurate notion,' he retorted, still looking hard at her. 'I'd give much to know who exactly it was who turned the lock on us in that devilish way! Evidently someone who went out of this room immediately after doing it, as anyone inside could scarce have failed to hear our shouts. Odd, don't you think, my dear sister?'

'Really, Francis!' reproved his mother. 'I should think you've done enough harm for one day without trying to pick a totally unprovoked quarrel with Lucilla! But I suppose in the circumstances you're a trifle overwrought, so we must excuse you. We shall question the servants, of course, as to who did lock the door; but you must realise that they were only obeying a longstanding order by doing so. No one can be blamed but yourselves for getting up to such schoolroom tricks.'

'I wonder?' murmured Francis, with a final cynical look at Lucilla.

Chapter XX

'Frank, you don't seriously think she would?' asked Ginny, incredulously.

It was several hours later and the two were driving to Misbourne House in Frank's curricle. Ginny was none the worse for her experience; indeed, she looked as fresh and charming as ever, having discarded the dirty riding habit and instead donned a carriage dress of red merino wool trimmed with swansdown.

He turned to look at her as she spoke, the admiration showing in his eyes.

'What, you mean Lucy? Don't mind telling you I'm confident she was the culprit. Mother says all the servants deny any knowledge of the business — besides, what would take 'em in there but household concerns which would be sure to occupy some time? Certainly long enough for us to have been heard. Stands to sense they wouldn't just go in, see the panel and close it, then come straight out again, don't it? Or if any of 'em did do that, why not admit it? As Mother was so good as to point out, they could scarcely be blamed for carrying out a rule of the household.'

'But Lucilla doesn't seem at all the kind of person to indulge in practical jokes,' objected Ginny.

'Perhaps not.' He paused a moment, then said a little awkwardly. 'Don't like to say such a thing of my own sister, but Lucy's got a spiteful streak, y'know. She was the one who locked Aubrey in there, all those years ago, only because they'd had some quarrel or other just before.'

'But my uncle said — that is, I thought he meant that you had played that prank on Aubrey?'

'Yes, well, no point in carrying tales, is there? Something schoolboys bar — especially when a girl's involved. Bound to get the worst of it, anyway, with girls,' he added, with a wry smile. 'They're always believed in preference to their brothers.'

Eugenia allowed this cynical philosophy to pass unchallenged. 'But even so — what grudge had she to pay off against either of us? If it really wasn't intended as a poor sort of joke, that is.'

'She's grudges in plenty against me, if she cares to recall 'em.' He looked at her sideways for a moment. 'But I don't fancy that was it.'

'Then what? Surely I have done nothing to annoy her? If so, it was unintentional, I assure you. I can't truly say that we are bosom bows, she and I, but at least we contrive to rub along tolerably together.'

He hesitated, appearing to be concentrating all his attention on his driving. Ginny was not deceived, however.

'Well?' she demanded impatiently. 'If you've something on your mind, Cousin Frank, speak out. I can't abide hints and roundaboutation — let me have a plain tale, for goodness' sake!'

He smiled down at her with an unusually gentle expression on his face.

'What a forthright little creature you are, my dear Ginny,' he said, softly. 'That's why you're no match for Lucilla.'

'We'll see that,' she retorted, spiritedly. 'But what do you mean precisely? In what way is she opposed to me?'

'I'm afraid it's a matter of property — you're poaching on her preserves, you see, if only unintentionally.'

'Poaching on her preserves?' He saw a light blush touch her cheeks, then she sat up very straight in her seat. 'I'll not pretend to misunderstand you,' she said, a little awkwardly. 'You mean — something to do with Sir Peter Martyn, don't you? That Lucilla didn't like his offering to accompany me to his home today?'

He nodded. 'That's it. She's moving in for the kill, is dear Lucy, and Heaven help anyone who gets in her way.'

She looked at him in amazement for a few moments, then burst out laughing.

'Oh, no! It's too ridiculous — you're gammoning me, aren't you?'

'Devil a bit of it. I know my own sister, right enough. She means to have Martyn this time round, and she's playing him for all she's worth. Shouldn't be surprised,' he added, reflectively, 'if she don't bring it off, too. Deuced attractive female, Lucy — got to admit that, though she ain't just in my style. I prefer —' he stole a look at her — 'quite a different type of girl.'

She was too taken up with the first part of this speech to pay any heed to the implied compliment.

'You speak as if the gentleman had no mind of his own,' she said scornfully. 'And that's not in the least as I understand him.'

'Ah, but then —' his tone was gentle again — 'you make no allowance for the force of a previous attachment. They were once very much in love, those two. Oh, yes, Lucy as well, without a doubt — but Lucy's heart isn't allowed to rule her head, as you may have seen for yourself. Different this time, though. She's caught her Earl and his fortune, and can now afford to give rein to her emotions.'

'You paint a charming portrait of your sister,' said Ginny, through lips that quivered slightly.

'You asked for a plain tale, sweet Coz,' he said lightly, as he turned the curricle between the wrought iron gates of Misbourne House.

She did not answer; indeed, she would have found some difficulty in doing so, for a pulse was beating somewhere in the region of her throat. The confusion of her thoughts was such that she did not know whether she most wanted to meet Sir Peter and explain her defection to him or never to set eyes on him again. What Frank had just said to her lay like a leaden weight on her spirits. It seemed to her at that moment that never again could she recover the tranquil mind she had brought with her to Buckinghamshire. As the curricle drew ever closer to the house, these feelings increased until it took the utmost self control on her part to mount the steps at the entrance without faltering, in spite of Frank's arm to assist her.

They were admitted to a pleasant parlour which overlooked the flower gardens at the rear of the house. Daffodils were nodding in the beds and clumps of crocuses gave splashes of colour along the borders. After a quick glance out of the window like one searching for a means of escape, Ginny's eyes returned to the room, where Lady Martyn had risen to greet them.

Of Sir Peter there was no sign. Ginny let out a little sigh; though whether of relief or disappointment she would have found it difficult to say.

Lady Martyn was all kindness and understanding when the unfortunate events of that morning were recounted to her. Like the good hostess and, moreover, the kind-hearted woman she was, she was more concerned to learn that Ginny had taken no harm from the experience, than in hearing apologies for something which she declared had been quite beyond her young visitor's control.

'Are you quite sure, my dear, that it was wise to come out this afternoon?' she asked Ginny, with sincere solicitude. 'A note would have done, you know, to explain matters — and, after all, ours was only an informal arrangement.'

'Oh, but I couldn't for anything have you think me so uncivil, ma'am! And then Sir Peter was put to so much inconvenience on my behalf — I felt I owed you a personal explanation, at the very least.'

'As for Peter, young men must have exercise,' replied her ladyship, with a laugh. 'It's no more for them to ride in one direction than another. What do you say, Francis?'

Frank agreed, and asked where Peter was at that moment.

'I believe you may find him round at the stables, if you care to step that way. But I can easily send for him.'

'No, no, I'll go after him myself, ma'am. I dare say you ladies may like to have a little time alone together.'

As soon as he went out, Ginny found herself in a flutter once again. She kept wondering if Sir Peter would return with Frank, and trying to calculate how long it was likely to be before they both appeared in the parlour. This gave her conversation with Lady Martyn a somewhat disjointed quality which rather disappointed that lady. She put it down, however, to Eugenia's unsettling adventures earlier in the day, and rang the bell for some tea to be brought to them.

'There's nothing like a good cup of tea for settling the nerves,' she pronounced, with the air of one making an important discovery. 'You'll see, my dear, it will make you feel more relaxed in no time.'

This prophecy was doomed not to be fulfilled, however. The tea arrived; no sooner had Lady Martyn poured out a cup and handed it to Ginny, than Frank and Sir Peter entered the parlour. Startled, Ginny looked up; her hand, blindly outstretched to take the cup, missed it, and an exquisite piece of Meissen china lay cracked on the table while hot liquid poured from it on to the Aubusson carpet.

'Oh!' cried Ginny in agony, and burst into tears, unable to control her pent-up feelings any longer.

'How clumsy of me!' exclaimed Lady Martyn quickly, making signs to the men over Ginny's bowed head that they should withdraw. 'There, my dear, it's no such matter, after all. It didn't go over your pretty dress, I trust? No? Well, that's all right, then — pray dry your eyes, and I'll ring for the housemaid to clear this up.'

Sir Peter had taken a step forward on seeing Ginny's distress, surprising himself by a sudden strong urge to comfort her. In response to his mother's signal, however, he drew Francis out of the room and into an adjoining one.

'Devilish awkward for the poor girl,' he said. 'I suppose we startled her, bursting in like that. Still, my mother'll soon settle matters. Can I offer you a glass of wine, Frank? Something stronger than tea is indicated, I think, don't you?'

Francis accepted, and Sir Peter busied himself at the sideboard.

'That wasn't it, Peter. Fact is, she was more than a trifle upset at the thought of facing you and Lady Martyn to apologise for this morning.'

Sir Peter paused in the act of pouring out the wine. 'But that's absurd — naturally, we should understand how unavoidable it all was. But I dare say Miss Eugenia may have been somewhat overset by her unlucky experience — can't have been pleasant for a female.'

'Damned unpleasant for me, too, if you want to know! But no, you've got it wrong, she wasn't in the least overset. Never saw such a cool hand in my life — game as a fighting cock! She's a fine girl, that one, and I don't mind telling you,' added Frank, as he accepted a glass from his host, 'that I mean to marry her, if she'll have me.'

Sir Peter gazed thoughtfully at his own glass. 'Yes, well, I collect that was always intended,' he commented, drily.

'Oh, I'm not thinking now of m'mother's schemes — this is on my own account. Grown devilish fond of Ginny. She's the only woman ever to make me contemplate matrimony, give you my word. I'd take her without a penny, and I can't say fairer than that, what?'

'No, indeed. And do you think she's prepared to take you?'

There was a sudden alertness about Sir Peter's expression now that did not escape Frank's eye.

'How can I say? We deal well enough together — laugh at the same things, share a dislike of humbug and overmuch formality. When we're together, we go along very pleasantly. But —'

He broke off. Sir Peter raised his eyebrows.

'But?'

'Oh, I don't know! I suppose there's more to it than that. I have a strong persuasion that she's not the girl to marry without her affections being deeply engaged, and whether I'm the man to do it or not, God only knows.'

Sir Peter smiled wryly. 'You are not without a certain reputation in such matters, I believe.'

'Pah!' Frank drained his glass with a contemptuous gesture. 'Bits of muslin and sportive widows? Not to mention errant wives, now and then, if the truth must out. They can't be compared to Ginny!'

'No, I rather think not.' Sir Peter's tone was dry again.

'The devil of it is, there's so little time to try and engage her interest,' complained Frank. 'She goes to London in less than a fortnight, and what's that in a delicate affair of this kind, I ask you?'

'There is love at first sight, or so I've heard.'

'I don't flatter myself Ginny took to me at first sight, or even second, old fellow. Matter of fact, I've been inclined to suspect —'

He broke off. Sir Peter raised an inquiring eyebrow.

'But never mind that,' Francis finished, abruptly. 'I suppose you're going to this ball of the Mandevilles next Tuesday?'

'I've accepted the invitation, yes.'

'Sure to be devilish slow, but there's no getting out of it, since Aubrey's engagement to Hetty Mandeville's to be announced,' remarked Francis, glumly. 'Still —' brightening a little — 'at least I'll be able to dance with Ginny. I wonder if they'll have the waltz? Now there's a dance that really does offer golden opportunities.'

'I very much doubt it. The Red Lion isn't Almack's, and even in that haunt of fashion permission to dance it is most grudgingly given, as you know. I fear the waltz would shock our neighbours here exceedingly.'

Francis was bound to agree, and thereafter their talk drifted on to sporting topics.

Meanwhile Eugenia had recovered her composure, apologised yet again to her hostess for this further social gaffe and was preparing to take leave.

'Do come again,' urged Lady Martyn. 'Have you any other days free for the remainder of the week? There's been no time to show you round today, but I think it might amuse you to see the Chinese room which my younger daughter Eleanor designed — she is quite talented in that way, though perhaps I should not be the one to say so. However, you may not care for that kind of thing, and I know you must have many other calls on your time at present.'

Ginny was grateful for the forbearance which prompted her hostess to welcome for a second visit such a clumsy visitor, so she tried to forget her odd reluctance to encounter Sir Peter, and answered that she would be delighted.

'I know we are all promised to the Mandevilles for tomorrow, ma'am, but I believe the day after is free. If you really feel no apprehension for your china after my clumsiness today —' with a little smile — 'perhaps I might come to you on Thursday afternoon? There is no occasion to offer me tea, you know.'

Lady Martyn laughed. 'That will be splendid. I shall look forward to it. And I think, if you'll permit, Miss Ginny, I shall send the carriage round for you. It may well be raining, for one can't rely upon the weather at this time of year.'

This was decided in spite of Ginny's polite protests, and a time fixed.

'And I undertake to be punctual on this occasion!' Ginny promised. 'I shall refuse absolutely to view any Gothic horrors, or other tempting sights!'

'I think you are very wise. A little of that kind of experience goes a long way, I am sure. Well, now, since you wish to be gone, I had best summon your cousin to escort you.'

So in spite of all that she had hoped and feared from her meeting that day with Sir Peter, a brief parting was all that took place between them.

Chapter XXI

When Lady Martyn's carriage arrived for Ginny on Tuesday afternoon, she had to suppress a feeling of disappointment at being helped into it by a liveried groom instead of Sir Peter. Until then, she had not realised how much she had been hoping he would come.

She found a cordial welcome awaiting her at Misbourne House, but soon learned that its master was absent, and unlikely to return home before dinner. As she would be gone long before that, all expectations of meeting him was at an end.

Oddly enough, the knowledge set her at her ease, so that she was able to give all her attention to her hostess, and enter into their conversation with lively interest. There would have been something so very unnerving in the thought that he was liable to walk in on them at any time. She took herself severely to task for this great foolishness, so unlike her usual poise, and reflected that it was high time she joined her godmother in London. The sooner she set a distance between Sir Peter Martyn and herself, the better.

Meanwhile, she accompanied his mother on a tour of the house, and found the rooms very light and pleasant, furnished for the most part in modern style. It seemed to her that Lady Martyn was unexpectedly anxious to learn her taste in decorating and furnishings, and to discover her opinion of what had already been done at Misbourne House.

'Of course, when my son brings home a bride, she will most likely wish to change most of this,' she said, 'And that is as it should be — indeed, I made many changes myself when I first came here.'

'But won't you find that sad?' asked Ginny.

'No, my dear, for I shan't be here to see the alterations. When Peter weds, I shall join my widowed sister in Oxfordshire, who has long been hoping that we might set up house together. There's no room for two mistresses in one household, don't you agree?'

'Perhaps not, though I think, like many things, it may depend on the people concerned. Is it likely —' she hesitated and stumbled a little in her speech — 'do you think — that is, do you expect that Sir Peter will marry soon?'

'I hope he will.' Lady Martyn gave her a warm smile. 'There is no happier state than a good marriage. If only he chooses wisely, I could wish nothing better for him.'

If only he chooses wisely, thought Ginny. Would it be wise to choose Lucilla? Perhaps not; but what had love to do with wisdom?

She shook her mind free of such thoughts impatiently, and asked if she might not see Eleanor's Chinese room. This intrigued Ginny very much. It was exuberantly gay; a red wallpaper patterned with trailing flowers made a striking background for furniture in bamboo and silk, Chinese figures on pedestals, a black lacquer cabinet and several large vases in Canton porcelain. On the mantelshelf stood a clock in white marble and ormolu in the form of a Chinese temple, and the chandeliers were ornamented with bead tassels.

'What a romantic room!' she exclaimed in delight. 'Your daughter has unusual, imaginative taste, ma'am.'

'Ah, well, she can't claim quite all the credit,' replied Lady Martyn, smiling, 'for the Prince Regent started the vogue by decorating some of the rooms in his Pavilion at Brighton after this style. I dare say you haven't been there yet, as I collect this is your first visit to the south since you were grown up? But I do hope that you will go later on in the season, for Brighton is such a gay place. I'm sure you would love it.'

Afterwards they returned to the small parlour on the ground floor to take tea, which Ginny accomplished this time without mishap. They were sitting chatting very comfortably together when a step was heard outside, and the next moment Sir Peter walked into the room. He was wearing riding breeches and a brown coat which accentuated his tanned face and fair hair.

'Peter! I didn't expect you back so soon. How fortunate that you should have come while Miss Eugenia is still here. Shall I ring for some more tea?'

He bowed to Ginny, offering his hand, which she took with commendable poise.

'No, thank you, Mother. I haven't yet managed to acquire your addiction to the brew. I'm sorry to have interrupted your chat, but my business in Chesham was concluded sooner than I thought.' He turned to Ginny. 'Has she been showing you the splendours of Misbourne House? And what did you think of the Chinese room?'

'Oh, I was charmed by it! It's like something out of a fairy tale,' replied Ginny, enthusiastically.

'I might have guessed you would be fond of fairy tales.' There was a twinkle in his eye.

'Now, do you mean that for a compliment or an insult, I wonder? But perhaps I would do better not to inquire.'

'Yes, for you'll find no satisfaction in my answer, I am sure. If I say it's a compliment, you'll refuse to believe I'm telling the truth; if an insult, then you will have every right to feel offended.'

She gave him a saucy smile. 'Oh, dear, I had no notion that you could read my thoughts so accurately, sir! But it's just possible, you know, that you could be wrong.'

'Very possible, in fact.' He hesitated, looked as if he would say more, then turned to his mother.

'Have you taken Miss Eugenia round the gardens?' he asked. 'It's quite dry underfoot and the air's surprisingly balmy for early April.'

'Oh, no, so far we have concentrated our energies indoors. But would you care to go, Miss Ginny? If so, I think perhaps I shall ask Peter to accompany you, as I'm a little tired after our tour of the house.'

Ginny replied that she would, and was escorted by Sir Peter to a door which opened on to a south facing terrace surrounded by a stone balustrade. They paused here for a moment to look out over lawns and flower beds before descending a short flight of steps into the gardens. Here they strolled around for some time, talking lightly and easily on everyday topics. Ginny found she had quite recovered from her earlier foolishness; evidently, she thought with a wry smile, Sir Peter was more formidable in his absence than when he was actually present. And yet she had never been at all shy of meeting him until these past few days; it was quite absurd. But for the moment she was radiantly happy in his company, and able to keep up a flow of sparkling nonsense to which he readily replied in kind.

By now they had passed through the gate in the wall which enclosed the flower gardens and were walking towards a small ornamental white temple perched on a rise. They had almost reached this when the sky, with the volatility of April, suddenly clouded over and a few heavy drops of rain began to fall.

'Confound it!' exclaimed Sir Peter. 'We're in for a wetting if we don't run for it — come on, Miss Ginny.'

He seized her hand and together they raced for the building, reaching it just as the shower came down in real earnest. Still holding her hand, he pushed open the door and pulled her inside. The abrupt movement threw her off balance. Releasing her hand, he put out his arms to steady her; and the next moment she found herself tightly clasped to him. She looked up into his eyes, which were warm and tender.

'Ginny!' he whispered. 'Ginny, I —'

He bent his head as though he would kiss her; she raised her face, her lips eager to meet his.

But suddenly, unaccountably, he straightened and his arms dropped away from her. She stood there looking at him, watching his mouth settle into grim lines. He turned away from her then, inspecting the velvet cushions which covered a low marble seat encircling the interior of the temple.

'I fear these may be damp,' he said, tensely, 'so perhaps you had better not sit down.' He walked over to the door again, carefully avoiding any contact with her, and stared out.

'I think it will clear in a moment. If you won't object to remaining here on your own for a few moments, I'll fetch an umbrella from the house.'

She made some answer, but she did not know what, racked by stronger emotions than she could readily master. He looked at her once, gravely and searchingly; then stepped out of the temple and sprinted across the grass in the already diminishing rain.

As soon as he had gone, she collapsed on to the cushions, damp or not she did not care, and gave way to a short burst of sobbing.

It was over in a few minutes. She found her handkerchief, dried her eyes, and tried to tidy away her emotions as quickly as she had restored her appearance to normal.

But why, oh why, had he not kissed her, as she was certain he had intended to do? What had come so inopportunely, so finally, between them?

Was it Lucilla?

For the next few days, she was to wonder this; to live over again that enchanted walk in the garden with its unexpected climax that had become an anti-climax. He had returned not only with an umbrella, but with a servant carrying a cape for her, so that any personal conversation was impossible, on their way back to the house. When they reached it, he had made his bow and left her in the care of his mother, to be conveyed home later in the carriage with the groom in attendance. Since then, she had not seen him, not even in church on Sunday. She had understood from his mother, whom she saw briefly after the service, that he was visiting friends for a few days.

Francis was very attentive to her, riding and driving out with her whenever she was not otherwise engaged and the weather proved suitable. She was most grateful for the entertaining company he provided, in contrast to the insipidity of Lucilla and the thinly veiled disapproval of Lady Turville. As she dressed for the ball on the following Tuesday evening, she reflected with relief that in another week she would be on her way to London and the affectionate welcome she was certain of finding there.

Nevertheless, she dressed with care in a sea-green gown of satin with a ruched flounce at the hem. A velvet ribbon of the same colour held in place a cluster of curls at the back of her head, while tendrils of hair framed her small, piquant face. Her eyes looked large and dark as she surveyed herself in the looking glass before letting Nancy drape a Norwich shawl about her scantily clad shoulders.

The arrival of the Turvilles at the ball was well timed, being neither so early that the room was very thin of company nor late enough for there to be a danger of their being overlooked in the crowd. Hetty was standing to receive her guests with her parents and two of her brothers beside her. She looked very fresh and virginal in a simple gown of white muslin, her face alight with happiness. For a moment, Ginny found herself envying the younger girl, and wishing that she could resolve her own difficulties as easily as she had those of Aubrey and Hetty. But she was determined that tonight she would forget all her doubts and disappointments in the sheer delight of dancing, which she always enjoyed.

Before long, several dances were bespoken, Francis insisting that he should be allowed to partner her in the first. Indeed, he would have monopolised her programme, but she was firm in refusing to dance more than two with him.

'I was taught, sir,' she said, with mock dignity, 'that any female who allows the same gentleman to partner her for more than two dances must be considered fast.'

'Ah, but it's quite proper when she and the man are related,' he reminded her.

'We may be related, but our acquaintance is quite recent, and in a case like that, I'm not certain that your rules apply,' she answered, laughing.

'Since when have you been so concerned with propriety, ma'am, I wonder?'

'Oh, since I knew you, of course.'

He made a mocking bow. 'Yes, of course, I am a model of that virtue. But come, the music is striking up — let's take our places in the set.'

He led her out and the dance began. It was while they were going down it that she caught her first glimpse of Sir Peter, looking very handsome in white knee breeches and a dark blue coat of excellent cut. He was dancing with Lucilla.

Ginny's steps faltered for a moment as her eyes followed them, but she made a quick recovery and was soon treading as light as air, and laughing with her partner. At one stage the movements of the dance placed her next to Sir Peter.

He bent over quickly and said 'May I hope that you will save one dance for me? I will come to ask you again when this one is finished.'

She only had time to smile encouragingly before they were separated once more; but her heart sang as she went on her way.

When the dance was ended, Francis led her to a chair in an alcove somewhat secluded from the ballroom by a row of tall potted plants. There was no one else in this retreat at present, and Ginny rather feared that Sir Peter might not readily notice her there.

'Should we not join my Aunt?' she asked, starting to rise from the chair.

'Not for the moment. There'll be another dance starting in a short while, and there's something I must say to you first.'

'Oh, very well.' Reluctantly she subsided into her seat again. 'What is it?'

He looked at her with eyes full of admiration; she guessed then what was coming, and felt a pang of dismay.

'I didn't intend to say it now, but, confound it, you look so enchanting, you're enough to turn any man's head! Ginny — lovely, adorable Ginny — I love you to distraction, you must know that I do! Say you care for me a little, dearest — say you'll marry me!'

He was leaning ardently over her, having taken her hands in his, when they both noticed a figure standing before them.

With a muttered curse, Francis hastily drew back and stood up to face the interloper.

It was Sir Peter.

'I appear to be intruding,' he said. 'I apologise.'

He turned on his heel and left them.

'Oh, Frank!' exclaimed Ginny, impetuously. 'Now look what you've done!'

'What have I done? Sent away one of your partners? Who cares for that? I only hope you will give me permission to send them all packing! But won't you answer me, Ginny? Say something, I implore you, for I can't bear this suspense!'

She looked at him with an affectionate compassion that he saw at once bore no relation to the love he felt for her.

'What can I say, Frank?' she asked, quietly. 'I know I should speak of the honour you do me, and indeed that wouldn't be an empty form of words, for I feel truly honoured to think that you wish to make me your wife. But —'

'It isn't your fortune, believe me, Ginny — I'd take you if you were a pauper — it's yourself I want — the adorable, bewitching you! I can't get you out of my mind — in all my life, I never felt for a woman like this — assure you.'

His words tumbled over each other in totally uncharacteristic confusion. She felt humbled and deeply sorry.

'I know that — I do you the justice to believe that you'd never have sought after me to capture my fortune. But I'm afraid it's no good. Frank. I respect you and am fond of you — as a brother, no more. I'm sorry, but so it is.'

'Can you give me no hope? If you are fond of me, as you say — and we deal famously together, Ginny, I'm sure we could be very happy as man and wife — then perhaps if I give you more time —' He broke off, making an effort to control himself. 'That's it,' he said, in a calmer tone. 'I've been too deuced sudden. I was trying to be patient, to give you long enough — but you look so lovely tonight, and suddenly I couldn't wait any longer. I've been a blundering fool. Forgive me.'

'There's nothing to forgive,' she said, softly. 'But I think I must make you understand that I can never change my mind. It's not a question of time, you see. I —'

She broke off in confusion. He looked at her searchingly, with pain at the back of his eyes.

'You're trying to tell me that there's someone else, aren't you? That you can never care for me, because your affections are already engaged?'

She nodded as a slow blush covered her cheeks.

'And I think I know who it is, too,' he continued, in a low tone. 'If I am right, then it's most likely, Ginny, that both of us, you and I, will love in vain. But I'll not pester you, dear, with unwanted attentions. Come, let me take you over to Mother. And don't let this avowal of mine trouble you in any way — behave towards me as you've always done. I swear I'll not abuse your trust, and will try to treat you only as the brother you're willing for me to be.'

Very much moved, she put her hand in his. He bent over and kissed it, then guided her back to where Lady Turville was sitting.

Sir Peter did not come to request the next dance, nor even the one after that. He danced with his neighbours' daughters, with Hetty, and again with Lucilla, yet still he did not come. Ginny, never short of partners, went through every dance with a desperate gaiety, careful at the end of each one to place herself in a readily accessible position in case he should wish to approach her. Several times he was so near that a few steps would have brought him to her side. She could not help but realise that he was deliberately avoiding her. Was it because he had overheard Frank's declaration and thought that she had accepted it, or was it because of Lucilla?

Frank took her in to supper. With the heightened perception of a lover, he sensed that something was troubling her, and soon came to realise what it was. Supper was a lengthy affair of several courses, followed by a formal announcement of the betrothal between Hetty and Aubrey with subsequent speeches. During an interval which was allowed for guests to rise from the table, Frank sauntered over to Sir Peter, who was standing alone at the time.

'Well, Peter, that's one member of the family about to be disposed of in holy matrimony. When is there to be a second, eh?'

'I should have thought,' replied the other, drily, 'that you could best have supplied that information.'

'I? What on earth gives you that notion?' Frank grinned ruefully. 'Oh, I see. Dare say you overheard me making a cake of myself just now with Cousin Ginny?'

Sir Peter nodded, tight lipped.

'Yes, well, I'd lead her down the aisle like a shot, but the devil's in it that she'll have none of me.'

The other's face changed. 'You mean she refused you?'

Frank nodded. 'Positively and indisputably old chap. She'd give me no hope, either — said she'd never change her mind.'

'I'm sorry — it's a damnable thing —'

'No use dwelling on that,' said Frank abruptly. 'Thing is, I collect from her manner that her affections are already engaged, so my case was hopeless, anyway.'

There was no doubt now that he had his friend's undivided attention.

'I suppose she did not say — that is, you've no notion who—'

'The thing is,' said Frank, neatly side-stepping this inquiry, 'when I asked you about a second member of the family to get hitched, I wasn't referring to myself — naturally, no need to ask *you* that — but to Lucy.'

'Why the deuce should you suppose I know anything of Lucilla's intentions?' demanded Sir Peter, almost angrily.

Frank looked hard at him. 'Thought the two of you might have made a go of it at last. Looked a bit like it since Lucy came home, I must say.'

'The devil it has! But you ought to know, Frank that there's no going back in affairs of the heart — nothing so dead as an old flame. But if you thought that, then —' He broke off. 'Hell and damnation, what a fool I've been!'

But not, reflected Frank ruefully, such a fool as he himself was, to make a present of the girl he loved to his rival.

The remainder of the supper party was a torment to Peter Martyn. He kept turning over in his mind schemes for securing a few moments alone with Eugenia, and failing to think of anything. And it was not until the ball was over that he found an opportunity even to approach her in company, to ask if she would come riding with him on the following morning.

Neither of them passed a restful night, yet when they rode off together the next day they seemed unable to talk of anything except trivialities. With no very clear idea of where they were bound, they found themselves eventually close to the Lydeard Arms, where Sir Peter suggested they might leave the horses for a while and walk a little.

They stood beside the pond, looking down into its cloudy waters.

Ginny wrinkled her nose. 'It's an unsavoury pool,' she commented. 'I shall never forget that day when you fished me out of it, all over weeds and mud and no doubt looking the most frightful sight!'

'You may not perhaps have been looking your best,' he conceded with a smile. 'But even then, I was beyond noticing it. I shall never forget that day, either, Ginny. Shall I tell you why?'

She wanted more than anything to hear, but could not find the courage either to say so or to look up into his face. She continued to stare at the ducks on the pond, and only the faint red in her cheeks gave any sign of encouragement to him.

He gave a quick glance about him. They had the place to themselves, apart from the ducks and some geese on the village green.

'It was on that day that I realised what you meant to me, Ginny. It was a shock — we'd only met once or twice. But when I spoke to you of Frank coming to value you for yourself, I knew it was the last thing in the world I would want to happen. Yet it did seem to me afterwards that he was indeed forming an attachment for you, and I fancied that you were beginning to reciprocate his feelings. My own you can imagine.'

'Yes — yes, I can.' Her voice was very low, and still she did not look at him. 'You see, I was — feeling exactly the same kind of thing over Lucilla.'

'Lucilla! That is past and done with long ago — you swept the last regret from my thoughts! But, Ginny, dearest — you do mean then that you care for me?'

She looked up at that, the answer in her eyes. His arms reached out and held her, she lifted her face for his kiss, and all else was forgotten.

The landlord of the Lydeard Arms had come into the courtyard at that moment. He paused to survey the scene appreciatively for a few minutes, then he went back in to his wife.

'Hey, Sally, you'd best get dry clothes ready and some coffee on the boil! There's Sir Peter out there with the maid who fell in the pond, and as far as I can see, they're like to fall in again any minute!'

A NOTE TO THE READER

It's wonderful to see my mother's books available again and being enjoyed by what must surely be a new audience from that which read them when they were first published. My brother and I can well remember our mum, Alice, writing away on her novels in the room we called the library at home when we were teenagers. She generally laid aside her pen — there were no computers in those days, of course — when we returned from school but we knew she had used our absence during the day to polish off a few chapters.

One of the things I well remember from those days is the care that she took in ensuring the historical accuracy of the background of her books. I am sure many of you have read novels where you are drawn out of the story by inaccuracies in historical facts, details of costume or other anachronisms. I suppose it would be impossible to claim that there are no such errors in our mother's books; what is undoubted is that she took great care to check matters.

The result was, and is, that the books still have an appeal to a modern audience, for authenticity is appreciated by most readers, even if subconsciously. The periods in which they set vary: the earliest is *The Georgian Rake*, which must be around the middle of the 18th century; and some are true Regency romances. But Mum was not content with just a love story; there is always an element of mystery in her books. Indeed, this came to the fore in her later writings, which are historical detective novels.

There's a great deal more I could say about her writings but it would be merely repeating what you can read on her website at **<u>www.alicechetwyndley.co.uk</u>**. To outward appearances, our mother was an average housewife of the time — for it was usual enough for women to remain at home in those days — but she possessed a powerful imagination that enabled her to dream up stories that appealed to many readers at the time — and still do, thanks to their recent republication.

If you have enjoyed her novels, we would be very grateful if you could leave a review on **Amazon** or **Goodreads** so that others may also be tempted to lose themselves in their pages.

Richard Ley, 2018.

Sapere Books is an exciting new publisher of brilliant fiction and popular history.

To find out more about our latest releases and our monthly bargain books visit our website: **saperebooks.com**